STAY UPDATED!

If you haven't heard anything from us in a while, it means you're no longer on our list.

So if you'd like to get updates on our new releases (And we have a lot of them!) please consider signing up here!

Newsletters not your thing? Consider joining our exclusive Facebook Group!

Second Edition reprinted in the United States of America
Rebellious Valkyrie Press, 2016
ISBN 978-1-943773-25-1 (eBook, 2nd edition)
ISBN 978-1-943773-27-5 (paperback, 2nd US edition)
ISBN 978-1-943773-46-6 (paperback, 2nd INTL edition)

Cover Design by Untold Designs Romance and Fantasy Covers
https://www.facebook.com/untolddesignscovers/

Copyediting by R.A. Weston
www.rawestoneditorial.com

Summary:

Timothy risked everything he had last year on love. Had he meant to fall? No. But it hadn't stopped him from colliding into Naima. When it ended, nothing felt the same.

Until she came back…

After a Providence-free summer, Naima is just about ready for anything. Except resisting Timothy.

It's only a matter of time before their feelings for each other get the best of them, but will they be on the same page or completely different chapters?

Next Chapter is a continuance to it's first in series Same Page

CHAPTER ONE

Six months later...

Naima

The bus to Pawtucket was a quiet ride if any. I'd only been back in Rhode Island a few days, so it'd been awhile since I'd considered Providence my home. I'd stuck around for the active school months, but come summertime, I'd gone back to NYC. It was nice being home over the summer but still, I was anxious to reconnect to Rhode Island.

Things worked out nicely. Lisette sublet my space while I'd been gone, but the leasing obligation was about to be up, so I didn't lose my cozy place. She'd even let me crash on the couch until the time came, free of charge. Even more good news, Symposium promised I'd have my old job back. Just in time to drop their *sea-bees*.

Despite the trains running on a hectic schedule, I'd decided to come back Labor Day weekend, conveniently the same weekend as the unofficial Symposium cookout. A little food, a little music, old friends, and hopefully alcohol. Those were all I needed to make the time perfect. I was pretty close with everyone I'd met in RI that all my friends back in Staten Island had seemed so basic in comparison.

But there was that one issue. That dilemma that'd be difficult to avoid.

It'd felt like so long since I'd seen Timothy, especially at an out-of-work setting. If I thought too much, I'd replay our last serious conversation in my head, which was the last thing I needed right now.

Timothy had broken up with his girlfriend of four years to be with me; if I had known, who knows what we could've been. He'd never thought to tell me while he was in Texas, when I'd had so many doubts about us. I was more pissed that he'd waited until after I'd ended things. Maybe I'd overreacted but could you really blame me?

It had gotten to a point where he called the shots, and I was just looking to take my life back. I was nowhere near in the right during the whole situation, but *I* at least felt guilty. I wasn't that selfish. I let the idea of Timothy having a girlfriend torture me to the point I hadn't felt worthy to be with him anymore, in any shape or form.

Maybe I just hadn't seen her as a real, live person until his decision to be with her came knocking on the door. It wasn't until then that it became painfully obvious that spending his birthday with her meant he wasn't spending it with me. I should've considered that scenario more, but at the time it was oh-so-clear.

How was I to know his plan was to be with me? If he would've given me a heads up, I'm sure I would've listened. But instead, we'd spent an awkward winter and spring, developing a strained work-only relationship and honestly, I'd been relieved to go away for the summer.

The guy I'd been seeing before I left, the one I'd been with at the skating rink, hadn't lasted that long. Outside of a few dates and decent sex, we weren't together more than two months, and I had no idea if Timothy had dated or reconnected with his ex in the absence of our relationship.

But if I saw him, it'd be better today. I'd have to face him eventually, and I didn't want any surprises. Everything we were—the silent treatment, the work-only talks, the avoidance—that was what we were now. And every fiber in my being hated it.

❧

The smell of burning meat, coal, and lemonade seared my nose upon reaching Martha's backyard. If she hadn't gotten her nickname from her name itself, she would've definitely gotten it by the way her house and backyard looked. Not too showy, but suggested a comfortable salary.

There were some folk I recognized. Others might've been family or new people at Symposium. But before I approached anyone, I filled my salad plate. I was at that "have a Snickers" boiling point, and to ensure the safety of others, *thou shalt not speak until fed.*

When I reached the serving table, I filled my plate with all I could eat. I was in the mood for macaroni salad, so it was a relief to see it'd already been eaten from. You can't just eat anyone's macaroni salad, and I wasn't trying to be the guinea pig. But it was half-gone, enough to prove its worth. I grabbed a beer from a cooler while I was at it. Not my first choice, but when it was free, you weren't picky.

"Hey, Naima! Glad you made it. I wasn't sure you'd be back soon enough to come," Martha said, sneaking up beside me.

"I wasn't sure I'd be either, but thank you for inviting me. Your home is lovely." And it was. One of the many Queen Anne-style houses on the street, with the cutest little bell tower patios in the front. Add in a big backyard? *Beyond gorgeous.*

"Thank you, girl. I'm glad you found it okay. I would've

picked you up, but I was afraid of leaving my husband alone and coming back to nothing but burnt food." We both exchanged small laughs. It was nice of her to have thought of me.

"It's cool. I'm just glad that I could make it. Really, thank you so much for inviting me."

"I'll let you mingle a little bit. Let me know if you need anything and have fun!" Martha said, trailing off into the crowd. I eyed Genesis and Emily, grateful for so much familiarity in one group.

Genesis laid eyes on me, and they widened with anticipation. "Girl, when did you get back? We missed you so much!" She and Emily engulfed me in a mutual hug. It was good to be back.

"Friday, but I've been settling in. Getting back into the grove of things."

Genesis reached out for one of my braids, dangling it between two fingers before letting it go. "Where'd you get your hair done? I'm feeling it."

I'd been rocking box braids all summer, but the fall was approaching, and soon they'd officially outlive their expectancy. I was thinking about taking them out soon but wasn't looking forward to the protein treatments that would have to follow. They'd rocked while they lasted and frankly, nothing beat getting up and being ready to go.

"Just some place in Harlem. Dime a dozen out there," I replied.

"They look so cute. I wish I could wear them without looking silly," Emily said.

I couldn't imagine her with any. Her hair was as bone-straight and blonde as it came. But I was sure some sort of braids would look good on her. Just not anything as intricate as box braids.

"Is Ruby here? I haven't seen her yet."

Emily searched the grounds, glancing over her shoulder once or twice to check if she'd missed anything. "We haven't seen her, but I don't think she was coming anyway."

I shrugged it off. "Oh, well. I'll just text her. Guilt her for not coming." Ruby was definitely my go-to but I was glad I'd gotten to know Em and Gen more outside of work. Sometimes I forgot Emily was only eighteen. She was more mature than me most times. And Gen? She was a hot mess. She always lived up to her moniker whenever she was around.

Katrina was visiting family in Lagos, so I knew she wouldn't be making an appearance either. In between gab sessions, I texted Ruby back and forth.

Me: *You suck. Symposium party. Invisible ass. Fighting evil by moonlight again?*

Ruby: *And not winning shit by daylight* 😴 *Sorry I missed you.*

Me: *It's cool. We just need to hangout. Hope to see ya soon!*

It was just then I spotted Timothy walk in. His hair was look-ing...*aww man*, his hair was looking hella-good. A new haircut did him justice. Shaved sides with a slight pompadour fashion. He looked...*sexy*. Fuck him for real for looking so good after all this time away.

He held the hand of a girl, but it wasn't what I'd thought or at least braced myself for. His goddaughter Brooklyn. The little girl I'd met when we missed that movie screening to hit up Dave & Buster's. She was as energetic as an eight-year-old might be with the promise of food. He led her to the serving table, and I did my best not to look their way. It was hard enough as it was.

Forty-five minutes went by as Em, Gen, and I bullshitted about past times at work. Genesis and I were a little too lively. Must have been the six beers between us.

"I have to use the bathroom," I told them. "I'll be right back."

The worst thing about drinking was the frequent bathroom visits. It took me a minute to find the first-floor bathroom, but I was so glad when I did. Holding it in was straight-up torture. Afterward, I washed my hands and checked myself in the mirror to make sure I fixed myself accordingly. No loose braids sticking out for the world to see. Eyebrows on fleek. *Showtime.*

I opened the door, and a little girl popped out of nowhere near the bathroom door screaming, "Naima!"

Her memory was good. She hadn't wasted time putting together where she'd known me from. I didn't expect her to know the difference between a friend and a *friend*, but she didn't seem to know Tim and I didn't talk much. I didn't want to hurt her feelings, so I bent down to meet her.

"Hey, sweetie. Did you get lost?"

She smiled. "I wanted to use the bathroom. Tim said it was okay if I went by myself."

I glanced back at the bathroom door, then her. "If you want, I can stand guard while you go." Brooklyn nodded, then closed the door behind her. I knocked once, just to make sure she was all right. "Just making sure you didn't fall in," I shouted from the other side.

"I'm okay!" she yelled back.

I small-talked with her while I waited, asking her about herself and if she liked the food. It came as no surprise she liked the macaroni salad. It was full of carbs after all.

"So you must be having fun, huh?"

"Only a little. Timothy is really boring today."

Why wasn't I surprised she'd mention him. He did bring her here. "Aw, I'm sure he's just trying to make sure you have fun." My words came out soft, but defensive, and I hoped she didn't notice. The toilet behind the door flushed. I made sure she washed her hands when she returned to the hallway.

"Now let's see if we can find Timothy for you." I didn't want to, but I wasn't going to leave her.

With just the mention of Tim, he materialized at the patio door. He was holding two cans of silly string, which I assumed were intended for Brooklyn. His soft smile faded when his eyes diverted to me. Brooklyn scattered behind me, cowering before the cans.

"Brook..." Tim continued in a singsong manner. "Why don't you stop hiding and take your silly string like a warrior."

"No! You'll have to get Naima first!" Brooklyn giggled, using me as her sacrificial lamb. I should've known something was up. She probably wasn't lying that she had to go, but it seemed awful convenient considering it hadn't been more than two seconds after me.

"It's okay. I can take it," I whispered to Timothy.

"Come on, Brooklyn. She might not want to get sprayed."

"You sprayed everyone else!" she yelled back. So now I was being singled out, too?

"Brooklyn, your dad is going to be here any minute to pick us up. We have to get ready."

Brooklyn seemed suspicious as she clutched the sides of my jersey and peeked over. "You're gonna trick me!"

"No, I'm not, Brook. You want us to leave you? You were the one who begged to come. And you called him not more than fifteen minutes later begging him to pick us back up. But it's okay. Martha said she wanted a new kid."

Brooklyn squeezed out from behind me, covering her face. Timothy didn't look quite convincing, but I'm sure he could fool a kid. "Let's go get your coat."

Brooklyn relied on trust and uncovered her face. When her guard went down, his spray cans went up, filling the hallway with her child-like shrieks. "Yeah! You think you're slick, huh? Think you can hide behind somebody and be safe?" Tim taunted, demolishing her sense of trust with streams of string.

It shouldn't have bothered me, but it did. *Think you can hide behind somebody.* I was officially *somebody*. That was worse than being nobody.

Timothy

"You're going to hell for doing that ish to my daughter, Tim," Rick barked from the driver's seat. I was busy plucking purple and pink silly string out of Brooklyn's hair in the backseat. It was a good thing her hair contrasted against it. It made it easy to see the string to pull it out.

"Dag, you act like it doesn't come out. Plus, she had it coming. Brooklyn was talking out her butt." I wasn't always successful at it, but I tried my hardest not to swear in front of her. I could care less about other people's kids, but she was who I wanted to be the best influence over.

"Did you have fun, Brook?" Rick asked, adjusting his mirror to face her without turning around. She crossed her arms over her chest, like she was mad or something.

"No!"

I buckled my seatbelt before Rick backed out of Kmart's driveway and took off. "But you're full, though. Don't act like you ain't eat," I teased. It hadn't been my plan to stay as long as we did. Symposium closed early that Sunday, and it'd been on the agenda to hop around to other engagements, but I figured I might as well make an appearance and grab a plate. Then Brooklyn wanted to come, and I couldn't say no, so Rick promised to pick us up in an hour.

I wish I'd known Naima was going to be there. I hadn't seen her since the start of summer. She looked good. *Too damn good.* Didn't you hate seeing someone look better than the last time you saw them? It'd only make things worse when she started back at Symposium. I knew she'd be back—I just hadn't counted on it during the cookout.

And of course Brooklyn blew my spot, but it's not like she knew we weren't friendly much these days. I hadn't wanted to embarrass Naima, so I'd played along when the situation arose. I was going to apologize, but by the time Rick showed up, Naima'd already left. I wasn't about to stress about it now, but fate always had a way of pushing you while you're down.

"Yo! Naima!" Rick yelled out the window.

"Dude, why are you yelling?" Although it was painfully obvious. My boys knew about my breakup with Sherri, but I hadn't exactly informed them about me and Naima's fallout. She stalked the sidewalk and only stopped when she heard her name called. She hadn't gotten far when Rick pulled up his car beside her.

"You're walking?" Like it wasn't obvious.

"Just to a bus stop," Naima said, trying to look polite without glancing at the backseat. I knew what was coming. Rick was like the dude of giving rides.

"You need a ride?"

Naima's shoulders slumped, Rick blind to her discomfort. "I'm fine. It's not really that serious."

"I don't mind if that's what you're thinking. You just live in West End, right?"

"I do, but I'm not trying to take you guys out of the way—"

"Girl, just get in the car," Rick interrupted.

Naima opened the passenger-side door and slithered in. "Dag. If there wasn't a kid in the car, this would be friggin' suspect," she said, securing her seatbelt. At least I was in the backseat. Otherwise, it would have been an awkward car ride.

"How come Tim didn't tell us you were back?" Rick asked, invasive as ever. Naima's gaze wandered as she stared blankly out the window.

"I'm sure it just slipped his mind."

"You here for good? Or just the year?"

Naima lifted her hand, followed by a dragged out "eh."

"I don't know. My roommate was telling me something about her lease being up this coming June and she wasn't sure whether she was going to renew. Even if I had plans to stay, not sure I could afford it on my own. Who knows, though? Not sure what the future holds."

Rick took the hint and nodded as they both came to the same conclusion. My boy was a conversation starter, so it was easy to fade into the background. I'd have to let him know the details later on, when Brooklyn wasn't in the car.

I wasn't trying to listen to the conversation in the front seat, but I caught the part where Naima wasn't sure if she planned on staying past her last semester. Seeing Naima was hard. Being around Naima was harder. There'd been so much I'd wanted to express that night that I hadn't. I'd been so deep in my emotions that I'd thought I'd just forget about it. Or, at the very least, be good at hiding it.

Maybe going separate ways hadn't been a bad thing. It hurt. But what would've hurt more was her leaving and me being in the same situation I was last winter with Sherri.

I'd been so busy placing my mind somewhere my body wasn't that, in a few short minutes, Rick pulled up in front of Naima's apartment. The same apartment I'd drop her off at every morning, after a late night sleeping over. The same apartment where we'd chill or cuddle when we'd had a few short hours before her roommate came home.

"It was nice of you to drop me off. You didn't have to. I was okay with walking," Naima said, closing the door behind her.

"Nah. Any friend of Tim's is a homie to me."

Naima stuck her hand in the backseat window. "Bye, sweetie. It was nice seeing you again."

Brooklyn pulled Naima's hand in, attempting to reach for a hug through the window. Naima finally waved goodbye and skipped to her apartment stoop. Rick waited for her to disappear behind her door before driving off.

Something about her leaving left me feeling some kind of way. Naima had said goodbye to everyone *but* me. Even now, we'd never really said goodbye.

And it sucked.

CHAPTER TWO

Naima

A few days before I returned to Symposium, I learned I'd be subject to another orientation. When I left this summer, I hadn't been there a whole year yet, so three months away technically meant I was a new hire, despite all my information being in the system. The upside was I didn't need to be trained, so I could start today if I wanted. *And I so wanted to.*

Orientation was held in Kmart's office, with exceptions for the winter time when the *sea-bees* came in droves and her office was too small to host them all. There were only four of us, max, so we buddied up around one table, waiting patiently for whoever was running this session.

I couldn't wait to stop being the "new" girl. I finally had some seniority over a few people. Rashawn to the left of me was from Groton, Connecticut, attending Brown University for the next few years, while Pilar to my right was a local looking for some extra cash for the fall and winter season. There was a guy across from me who didn't talk much, and because of that, I knew he wouldn't last long. People here were anal about customer service, so we were expected to go above and beyond to make people happy. It was easy to do that in a bookstore. You give someone a book they were dying to get their hands on for months and you became their best friend. But even that had to start with an outgoing personality, and judging by how well the other three of us hit it off, he was definitely lacking.

"Sorry, everyone. I got caught up with some morning shipments and only had one person in the cafe with me. I promise this won't be long. Just some quick videos, a review of your paperwork, and did Martha give you all a training schedule?"

My heart sank. I thought I'd have at least a morning without calamity striking, but in came Timothy with his clipboard and sexy hair. Why was I being tortured this way? How many times would I be ignored before he acknowledged my presence? I looked to the clock on the wall, and it read 9:08. Just fifty-two minutes more of this unpredictable morning, and I'd be out of this office, away from this awkwardness. Away from Timothy.

He recited this whole introductory speech about what it was like to work at Symposium, and although he paraphrased it, I'm sure he read it off the same script or something. Including my interview last year, this was my third time hearing it. I was grateful when he popped in the first DVD, which took up twenty minutes, leaving only twenty more of this godforsaken nightmare.

He opened the floor for questions, making me feel left out since I had none, and also made us fill out additional paperwork. Tax forms, signatures, emergency contacts. The usual when you're offered a job.

"Okay, so I have one more video. It's about eight, nine minutes, give or take. But good news, after this one you're free to leave if you don't have any additional questions. *Cool?*" He popped in the video and took a seat at Martha's desk. His fingers glided across the keyboard, not giving a second thought to what any of us did in the background. I took out my phone to send a quick text to Ruby asking her if she worked today and, if so, which department. Sure, I'd seen some familiar faces on the way in, but I missed my boo.

Ruby: *I come in tomorrow at noon, but I think Butter Cookie comes in at ten. No longer a minor. They grow up so fast.*

At least I wouldn't face the day alone. The credits rolled as we reached the end of the video. The guy who didn't talk much rushed out before the rest of us could get out of our chairs, and just as I got up with plans to throw my crap in my locker, Tim called out to me.

"Naima, could you stick around? I have to talk to you for a second."

My heart pounded in my chest. He'd addressed me by my name, not my moniker. A huge step up from our last encounter at Martha's house. I couldn't count on us to be best friends, but I hoped this season would be better than spring where we barely talked at all. I was ready to be over this. I hoped he was ready, too.

I sat down in the chair closest to the desk, watching him type away in a program I'm sure only made sense to whoever accessed that computer. "Sorry, I'm getting the hang of all this new stuff. Since you've been gone, they've been grooming me for Buzz Lightyear's position. He's leaving in December, so I've only had a few weeks to prepare and there's still a whole lot of shit I have to learn. Thanks for your patience."

My stomach flopped hearing the news that Buzz was leaving. Buzz was the manager I'd worked the closest with last semester since the floor was his domain. Overall, he was a pleasant person, so I wondered where he was going and why no one had mentioned it at the cookout. I'd have to ask him for the rundown the next time we crossed swords, but how cool was it that Tim would take his place? Even if we weren't talking, it didn't mean I couldn't be happy for him.

"Congrats!"

"Thanks," he replied, not tearing his eyes away from the screen. I couldn't force a real conversation to happen. Maybe that was just how it was going to be from now on with us. If there ever was an *us*.

He spun around in his chair, a wisp of his musky cologne assaulting my senses as I prayed this would be over quick. It was hard to be this close to him, yet so far away. I was ready to lose myself in work, even if only to get my mind off it for a few hours.

"So welcome back! You came back just in time—lots to do, lots to learn. Um…so far you're the only one we've hired who's not seasonal *sooo*…I regret to inform you that where you were last spring is flooded with *sea-bees*."

My brows knit together, wondering what that had to do with me. As if he read my mind, he continued to clarify his statement.

"Meaning the only place to put you is the front end, and I know everyone hates being there or the cafe. If you prefer the floor, I think something may open up if one of the *sea-bees* doesn't work out, but for now that's what it looks like."

Just great. Not that it mattered where I went—Tim would still be the person I reported to. If I chose the front, I'd have a few months free from seeing him all the time, but come December, he'd be replacing Ravinder. If I chose the cafe, that meant most of the days I worked this season would involve us having to closely interact. Either way I was screwed.

"Do I have to let you know now?"

He nodded. "I haven't even finished your paperwork yet, so if you were trying to start today, I would really need to know now. Here's the deal—I'm not going to need you there every day. Just maybe seventy-five percent of the time."

I sighed. "The cafe's cool." Because three and a half months was better than five.

He stuck up two thumbs and reached over the desk to jot something down. "Okay, so I just need your license because the one we have on file for you expired this July and… Let me see what else I'm missing." He opened up a folder as his eyes darted over the files. "Oh, and I need an updated version of your availability, as well as your direct deposit forms if that's changed since the last time. But other than that, you're good to go."

He photocopied my ID and handed me back copies of everything that was in my work file.

"Think you could start at…" He glanced at his phone. "Well, it's a quarter past ten now. You want to start at eleven? You could leave at four, five, or even six. It's up to you."

I chose to stay until five since, between the shift and orientation, that would put me at seven hours. Six was pushing it, but I was willing to stay if they needed me.

"So you're all set to go. Thanks for bearing with me."

I offered a small smile. Although we weren't really talking, we were *kind of* talking. He may have even smiled back at me. Maybe it was the nerves getting the best of him for getting thrown into a new position. Either way it was a start. I took one last peek at my phone before I shut it off and shuffled my way to the door.

"Oh, and Staten Island?"

I stopped at the sound of my sobriquet.

"Happy belated birthday." That time he did smile.

Timothy

"Yo pass me some of that um…that um…" Marv snapped his fingers, as if by doing so the name of the item would flow from his fingertips.

"Dawg, you mean this barbeque sauce?" I corrected.

"Yeah, that."

I handed him the bottle and watched him drown what looked like a perfectly good meal in layers of barbeque sauce.

"Man, gross. I don't know how you're going to eat that now."

"Easy, like this," he said as he stuffed a hefty serving of rice, lamb, and whatever else the sauce had destroyed into his mouth.

"I swear, Marv. This is why I never eat around you. I stay losing my appetite."

"Whatever. So I like a little barbeque sauce on my food. It ain't hurtin' nobody. Hey, did I tell you about how I lost my phone the other day at Six Flags on one of those rides? Shit cost me seven hundred to replace. I don't care who's going to be there, who's paying, who's driving. Next time someone even mentions that place, I'm saying no." He always rumbled in Spanish at the end of his arguments as if to solidify his point, and no matter how long I'd known him, I'd never been able to catch a single word. I was sure none of it made sense to you unless you were Dominican, but I caught at least that he was pissed.

"So Rick told me your homegirl's back."

I stuffed a handful of fries in my mouth, unwilling to answer the question. All my friends knew about our *"relationship,"* but when it had gone south, I hadn't mentioned it or why. There were things you chose to talk about and other things that hurt too much to breathe life into. I knew if I'd told them what went down, they'd question me constantly, and at the time I wasn't ready to be grilled like that. Still wasn't.

"Rick said she was still bad, too. Umph. I would've wifed that up and then some." *So he says.* "I know you have to be hitting that up again. If that was me and we ended things on friendly terms, soon as she's back in town, we're cuffed up."

"Yeah, it's not like that right now. I think she's dating some-one," I lied—or rather, I think I did. She'd only gotten back a few weeks ago and hadn't shown up to the cookout with a date. To me, that spoke volumes.

"Damn, that sucks. It seems like ever since you broke up with what's-her-name—"

"Sherri?"

"That's it! Ever since you broke up, you've been all woe is me. Have you even tried getting out there? Dawg, you rusty."

As much as I hated to admit it, I hadn't even tried talking to another woman. Not since my breakup. Not since Naima. I'd been so busy with work, I hadn't had time to set my sails on any women. A part of me liked it that way. I'd been in a relationship so long, I'd forgotten what it was like to be single, and while I didn't prefer it, I just needed to be by myself right now. Even if that meant I wasn't getting laid. Not my choice, by the way.

"When was the last time you got some?"

I laughed. "Bro, you don't even want to know," I said, cowering in my chair. A few months was where I reached my breaking point, but this time I wasn't really thinking about hooking up with someone. Or, at least, that's what I convinced myself.

"I don't know. I still think you should hit up your homegirl Naima. Like, at least see what's up. She might have a man, but she was with you even when you weren't single."

Funny how he couldn't remember the name of the girl I dated for almost five years, but Naima he could remember at the drop of a hat. He was weird that way. He only remembered the stuff he wanted to.

I glanced at my phone. "We might have to grab that check. I have to be back in like eight minutes."

"You're good, Tim. I got this one."

"Oh, good look, fam. I'll see you…."

"Sunday."

"Right, Sunday." But, to be honest, since the mention of Naima's name, I'd already forgotten what was happening Sunday.

CHAPTER THREE

Naima

I tossed and turned all night on the couch, unable to catch one minute of sleep knowing what was going on behind our bedroom door. It wasn't as though I wasn't used to Lisette having company over or sexing the night away. When I thought about the few times when she was considerate of my sleepovers, I had no leverage to complain. But it was *who* it was with that had me messed up. My best friend in Rhode Island. My number one partner-in-crime. Miss Ruby Jiang-Cruz.

I'd felt some vibes coming from them a while back, but I certainly hadn't expected anything to come from it. Apparently the two hooked up over the summer, and while Lisette had spent nearly half the year saying she didn't have the time for a girlfriend, she'd made the exception for Ruby. She'd slept over the past three nights, while I'd slept on the pullout, bitter and resentful every time I was subjected to hear them in all their passion only reminding me that I hadn't had sex in seven months. And it'd been a *long* seven months.

I could already predict it. I was going to be that third wheel that didn't fit or somehow made the ride rougher. I was glad they were happy, only feeling some kind of way because I was close to both of them. There went the days where it would only be two of us hanging out. Now, it would always be the three of us.

A few minutes passed as Ruby tiptoed out of our bedroom in just a bra and panties, clothes folded across her forearms. I teased her by imitating her moans from last night, and she rewarded me with a middle finger in the air. I stuck my tongue out as she jumped on the couch, her elbow catching me in the stomach, destroying whatever sleep left there was to be had.

"Oh, shit, my bad. For some reason, I thought you had a pillow under there."

I pulled off my comforter, revealing a bright red tank top with matching flannel pants. "*Ugh*, what time is it?"

Ruby grabbed my phone from the dresser and read me off the time. "Almost six-thirty."

Lucky us, we had an early morning work meeting to go to, and neither one of us really got any sleep. Since she was already here, we both thought it best to go in together, which I was grateful for. At least I wouldn't be the only one walking in deprived of sleep.

"I have to take a shower, though. Do you want to go in before me?" she asked.

I volunteered to go second, needing a minute or two to decide how I was tying up this hair. I may have had two more weeks in me to prolong these braids and if I could help it was going to leave them in until my mother shipped me the hair steamer I'd left behind. I went with one of the dozen of Dutch wax print scarves I had lying around, knowing that if I wore a scarf, It'd break the monotony of choosing to wear the style down every day. I hated for my hair to look the same every day, something I didn't have a problem with when my hair was out.

#naturalhairproblems

Ruby gave me the heads up when she was out of the shower,

and I grabbed a towel from the hallway closet as I headed straight for the bathroom.

"I'm so jealous how precise you do your makeup," Ruby complained as we waited at the bus stop. "I swear wherever I try to wear lipstick, I never look better. Or maybe I'm not choosing the right colors. I want to look my age. I'm tired of going out with Lisette and I'm the only one who gets carded."

She was twenty-five but could seriously pass for nineteen. Must've been that Filipino blood. Wasn't sure why she was sweating the age thing, though. I didn't wear makeup to look younger or older. I did it because it was fun. Plus, it made me feel a little more confident walking out the house. That was a definite plus.

"Ruby, you can wear whatever you want, but if you don't feel good about it, it's going to show through. Here." I grabbed her face by the chin, examining her flawless tan skin and making note of her full lips and amazing eyebrows. "Start with orange. It sounds out there, but if red and pink are too tame, orange is the way to go."

The bus pulled up in front of us right on schedule, leaving us enough time to get a stab at the good stuff before the cafe was left with decaf coffee and finger foods no one else wanted.

A huge whiff of Roasted Nut Delight made me gravitate to all the options they laid out on two of the reserved tables. It was only the best for Symposium employees, and I was grateful for selections outside of Dunkin' Donuts. *I hated their coffee.*

It was a packed meeting with forty-odd people. I hadn't even realized this many people worked here. In the week I'd been back, I'd only worked alongside friends from before I left, but already I was super cool with the ones from my orientation. Except for that one quiet guy who wouldn't last.

Angel and I fought over the last corn muffin, agreeing to split it down the middle since we'd brushed hands reaching for it. At twenty-one, he was such a sweetheart with his dimples, bronze skin and hooded eyes. When we'd met last year, I'd really misjudged him for being full of himself and cocky, but he was the complete opposite. A big teddy bear. Plus, he totally followed through when I told him he could sing to me anytime. Romeo Santos had nothing on him, and I loved me some Romeo Santos.

"Naima, you should get your cousin a donut," Katrina said, seated all the way across the room.

"Oh, I didn't know you two were cousins," one of the newer girls declared.

By blood, we weren't. But it was hard explaining to people that your moms could have gone to the same salon back home and considered each other family because of it. That and you addressed friends of parents as uncle and auntie. Despite being born in the states, in a house with Nigerian parents from the home country, those were just things you didn't question. Come to think of it, there weren't many things you questioned. Nigerian parents were always right, even when they were wrong. To sum it up, I was never the envy of any of my friends.

The second Timothy walked in with Ravinder, I knew we were starting soon. For a bookstore, we sure had a lot of meetings, but it was the beginning of the school year, the store's busiest time, so I suppose they needed to line all their ducks in a row. Meetings were always the easiest part of the day, so I wasn't complaining. Timothy laid down a box of what looked like books and prizes, most likely for the winner of Customers' Favorite Week.

Customers' Favorite Week was a contest they ran the first week back to school where they had the customers fill out these questionnaires about the employees after doing their last-minute shopping. The employee who won chose the book of the month for September all the way through December. They also got a picture taken each month with their current choice that would advertise all over the store, a flashy Customers' Favorite nametag, and a one-hundred-dollar Visa gift card.

Bruce won last year, so for the four months in question, he'd had everyone reading cheesy yet steamy M/M erotica. Imagine the book discussions we'd had over those. It managed to do two things, though—turn them into bestselling books for those months at Symposium and put aside my biases against M/M romance. I still loved my contemporary, though, but it was a chance for me to expand my reading tastes.

Ravinder set up a PowerPoint presentation on one of the back tables, and signaled for Timothy to start while he tested the slides.

"As you know, it's back-to-school month at Symposium. Some of you are new," he said, pointing to the flood of new faces. "Some of you are not, but my goal today is to get everyone up to speed about how September's going to look and how the fall season is going to go." His presence commanded the room as he continued.

"The game plan is to make this season successful, with record-breaking numbers. We are in direct competition with those chains we do not name in these walls, but we do something extraordinarily different than those other bookstores. We learn names. We build relationships. We go above and beyond to help people find that perfect book they've been looking for. We hire handsome devils like me who can talk people into buying anything."

A roar of laughter filled the room, waking up whoever wasn't already fully awake by now.

"But really, though, we're community-based. Indie. The underdogs. So that means we don't have to try harder—we strive to. The better we do this season, the more hours we can budget. The more hours we can budget, the more money for all of us. Doesn't that sound fantastic? Now onto our lesson plan."

He handed the floor to Ravinder, and my heart skipped a beat when he sat down next to me.

Since I'd been permanently placed in the cafe, our conversations consisted of the following: "*Good morning*" and "*See you tomorrow.*" Oh, and how could I forget the occasional "*Ready to go on break?*" Other than that, we didn't find much to say to each other. My guess was that both of us were mentally debating whether it was even okay to do so. At least he could sit next to me. I wanted this season to be better than last spring.

The presentation consisted of updates to the stores procedures, a change on the return policy, and how they were preparing for special events in the next few weeks. Most things they brought up last year about this time, but with Timothy putting that public relations degree to work, it sounded far more exciting this year.

"Good news, everyone. Sales are up seventeen percent from last year's back-to-school opening week, so it looks like I'm doing a good job—*ahem*—we're doing a good job. Can I get a drum roll please?"

A few of the others started drumming the tables and I, feeling in high spirits, joined in.

"So, now, the moment you've been waiting for. The winner of Customers' Favorite Week is…" Tim tore open an envelope, his eyes lighting up as they bounced in my direction. "*Miss Staten Island.*"

The hate was real today. Everyone wondered how the girl who had only been back a week could have the Customers' Favorite title bestowed upon her. They even accused Tim of rigging the results, but seeing how we weren't even tight like that anymore, all I could do was laugh off the jealousy that oozed from everyone in the room.

"Now before everyone goes ballistic, Staten Island won by a landslide. No one even came close to her numbers. Allow me to read off the stats. Book recommendations: one hundred and twenty-seven. Purchases based off those recommendations: seventy-four. For the food bank donations we were sponsoring, the girl sold one hundred and eighty dollars' worth of tickets, which means she was asking everybody. Are you all asking everybody?"

"She speaks like six languages. Of course she's asking everybody," Emily spat.

But all I did was stick out my tongue and accept my many gifts.

"I only ask the folks that look like they *want* to donate," said Bruce. "If they're buying from the bargain section, that's a sure-fire way to get me not to ask. I hate it when people ask me."

"You guys, *you have to be asking everyone*. Some people surprise you. Plus, Staten Island always gets the sweetest notes written about her from customers. So take this as a chance to step your games up."

I fished through the box of books to examine January through August's books of the months, deciding I wouldn't read all of them due to personal taste and time restrictions if I wanted to keep my GPA up in this final year. (Arabic looked like it'd be kicking my ass this semester.)

"Butter Cookie, catch!" I threw her some young adult contemporary as she fake-cried in appreciation. I let a few others take their pick of the ones I knew would just collect dust, leaving me with just three books. A contemporary, a memoir, and a middle grade book all from authors who had been on my radar for months.

Because of my summer back home, I'd missed the chance to have a surprise birthday party in my honor, but this was better anyway. After months of home-cooked meals, the last thing I needed was birthday cake, but it was sweet when I'd got a picture card in the mail from everyone just in time for my uneventful birthday. The only person and signature missing was Timothy's, but that didn't really surprise me.

"Don't forget. You have to pick a book of the month," Tim announced as everyone started getting up from their seats, those of us who were on after nine were anxious to start the work day.

I blurted the first thing to come to mind. "Uh…how about *Bad Feminist* by Roxanne Gay?"

Timothy whispered a thank you. "Finally, a book I actually want to read. I can already tell I'm not going to regret you being the customers' favorite."

Wait, had he just said more than five words to me? At one time? What could I say back? Did it even require a follow-up comment? Think, Naima, think. Say something before the moment was gone.

"Yeah, bro," I said in a wobbly voice that didn't sound anything like mine. I didn't even say "bro." Hell, neither did anyone I know. Nice going, Naima. You killed that one.

When Emily strolled onto the cafe floor, I thanked the stars I was getting off at three. I'd been here since the morning meeting and had a stack full of school assignments I'd put off all week. I'd managed to snag a few morning classes back-to-back on Monday and Wednesday. Tuesday was my other day, with just one night class, so whatever coursework I had had to be finished by the end of this weekend. That only left me a day and a quarter.

This year was Emily's first at Rhode Island College. While we didn't see much of each other there, we were two proud attendees, mutually repping that Anchormen pride.

"I think I'm going to kill myself over this first week of classes. Here I am thinking they slow down and explain everything to you. I've already bought, like, three books out of the *Books for*

Dummies series. One on college algebra, one on technical writing, and another on Spanish. I'm not sure why it's even required to take languages anyway. I'm not using that shit. I'm an arts major. *Arts...*"

#firstworldproblems

"Sweetheart, you aren't getting any sympathy from me. You know what I have to take this year? Arabic. Consider Spanish a blessing. Everyone knows even a little Spanish. Plus, didn't you take it in high school?"

She grimaced. "Kinda. *Sorta.*"

"Either you did or you didn't."

"Okay, look. It was the only class I had with all my friends. I don't even know how I passed it."

And that was exactly why, when I had the opportunity to learn other languages, I did so out of the country. It was the only way to truly become fluent if you didn't grow up speaking the language. If you didn't want to starve, you sure as hell had to learn.

I laid a hand on her shoulder, reassuringly.

"Que te vaya bien, blanquitita."

She chuckled. "I don't know what any of that means."

"Butter Cookie, you better not be taking no days off. And you know I'm always here if you need help. Language major, recuerdas? See you Tuesday, babe." I rid myself of my apron, making sure to unclasp my brand-new fancy nametag. Sure, it was kind of corny, but it was a reminder of how helpful people found me, something I didn't hear often.

I sprinted through the store's main floor, ecstatic to finally see that time clock when I reached the back near Martha's office. *I was so ready to leave.*

My fingers zoomed across the keypad as I punched my numbers in the device and let out a sigh of relief to see my surname and employee number next to the words, *Punch-out Successful.*

"Hey, I'm glad I ran into you. I was trying to catch you before you left." Tim stood in front of me with a book in his hand and a camera around his neck. "I have to get your picture for the September Book of the Month displays."

Damn, did it have to be today? My lips were already colorless and chapped since I hadn't been smart enough to bring the lipstick I'd started the day with or some Blistex to keep them moisturized. Plus, this scarf on my head I had to constantly read-just because of how hot it was. I wasn't looking as presentable as I was this morning and while no one else would know this wasn't the initial plan for it, I would know. *I would.*

He had me stand up against the wall and took three pictures before he suggested going in a different direction.

"Okay, so these are all nice pictures, but I don't know… You sort of have a one-of-a-kind personality. I want that to sell the book."

For a second, it was hard to imagine that we'd ever stopped talking. That we weren't just coworkers who'd had that misunderstanding way back when. This was the first time in weeks he'd ever said anything remotely complimentary. Sure it wasn't exactly noteworthy or even blush-worthy, but I couldn't help the smile that formed on my lips. I held the book to the side of my face, awe transforming my quirky expression.

His smile beamed. "That's perfect." He snapped a photo, offering to let me see it before it went official, just in case I hated it, but it worked. Whimsical and one-of-a-kind, just like this bookstore.

"Thanks for your time," he said, walking away before I could add any kind of "You're welcome."

CHAPTER FOUR

Timothy

With a half an hour to kill, Angel and I laid across the only two couches the break room provided. Had I had been alone, chances were I would've chosen this time to catch up on much needed sleep, but the situation changed when you had a break buddy. Too bad there wasn't shit to do and neither one of us had food to eat.

That being said, these twenty-nine minutes wouldn't be a total loss and with break-time boredom setting in, we only had one of two options. Either we'd choose to sit there silently, our eyes glued to our phones. It was easy to forget what it's like to have much needed human conversation. *Or,* we typically chose to play a quick game of *'this or that'*.

Anyone that entered the room was invited to play, but seeing how it was just the two of us, it looked like it was going to be one on one.

After three death match rounds of a rock-paper-scissors, Angel won the right to pick the first topic.

"Woman and dating."

I scratched my temples. "C'mon man. Pick something easy like sports." Because discussing either subject was never easy.

"I won. I call women and dating."

I let out a heavy sigh. "Fine. Just if any women walk in, we can't ask questions like *fat ass or big breasts*. Tame, dawg. Keep it tame."

"Time's a wasting. Hit me with that first question, Timbaland." I searched my thoughts, blurting out the first thing to come to mind.

"*Uhhh*, street smart or book smart?"

"Street smart. Good in bed or good conversationalist." *Fuck.* This one had me.

"*Ehhh…skip.*"

"Timbaland. *You can't skip.* You know the rules."

"*Urgh*. Alright then, good in bed." Because to this date, I hadn't met any woman who was good in bed and a *bad* conversationalist. *My turn.* "Selena or Amara La Negra?" He shifted on the couch to look in my direction.

"What you mean like music?"

"Dude, c'mon. You're the one who chose the topic. Of course I don't mean no damn music." He shuffled in his spot like a little kid unable to get his way.

"As a Dominican, for me to say anyone other than Amara La Negra would be blasphemous, so Amara. *Urgh*, that was dirty. Home-grown or foreign born." Speaking of home-grown…

Plastic bag in hand, Naima walked into the break room and towards the one of two microwaves in the corner. Not that I was looking or anything—but if I were, I'd be the first to admit that even though her own hair looked good on her, the length of the braided extensions were working. They stopped right where they needed to. Right above her ass—which looked sexy by the way, in her tight denim jeans. You know, *if* I was looking that is.

"Oye Mi Negrita, como tu' ta?" Angel asked interrupting our little game.

"To' ta frio, loco. Tu lo have." She answered back in that same island-like twang.

"What you got to eat over there?" Angel asked, this time in English. She turned around scrunching her nose up.

"Just some stuff my dad helped me cook yesterday. This is my first ever attempt at Apon soup. You might not like it but there's a lot here, if you want some." Forgetting I was here, Angel got up to stalk Naima in the corner. There goes our game.

He hooked his arm around her neck and kissed her on the top of her head. The guy was so tall, I don't know how he ever dated women as short as Naima was.

"Oh, and you got some plantains? What's good, Naima? You going to eat them all? I know how you girls be about y'all diets. I could take care of that for you, mama." She pushed him away from her, her smile faltering when she turned back to me.

"Hey Tim, want some?"

"Damn, so we have to split it three ways?" Angel complained.

"Boy, shut up! I don't have to be offering you nothing. Ungrateful self." In the midst of all their bickering, I found myself a seat at a nearby table.

"Sure, I'll try some." She handed him a two bowls of something that now cooked, the smell had lingered throughout the room. It looked more like a stew than a soup with its thick texture but there was something I remember her saying in the past about how Nigerians had what they called 'eating soups' and drinking soups'. This one looked like an eating soup. From first taste, it was fucking amazing.

"Hey Du-wop, before I forget. You cut hair, right? My father and stepbrother were visiting for a few days. My stepbrother, he's like sixteen and into all that trendy hair mess. He wants a place to get his hair cut before he leaves. Says he didn't know there were going to be so many pretty girls out there, or whatever. I forget what he said, the little brat. Anyways, when do you usually work there?"

"Shit, every day except Sunday. I usually leave at like three, though. Tell him to come in before then. I'll hook him up."

"Do you have a portfolio or something? Just to get an idea if that's what he likes." He pointed to me with his lips.

"Just look at Timbo. When he's not on some lazy shit, I always cut his hair." Suddenly I felt self-conscious when her eyes traveled across the table. Staring at me. Judging me. And looking so damn beautiful doing it. If I could put into words how it felt to have her assess me, I'd have to confess that there weren't any words, only feelings.

"Okay, Du-wop you sold me. Timothy's hair always looks nice. I trust you." A small smile fought its way to the corner of my mouth.

Maybe it wasn't as forward as saying, "Hey handsome, what do you say to us getting out of here?" but still, a huge boost to the ego, none the less. I peeked at my watch.

"As always, it was a pleasure spending break with you, Du-wop. Staten Island, thank you for feeding me. Your culinary skills are definitely something to fuck with. Until next time, people." I pushed my chair from the table, throwing away my empty paper bowl on the way out. But not before stealing a look to catch those sexy eyes glancing back at me. No words, just feelings. And this feeling, I must say, had me hella-high.

Naima

"Oww!" Ruby cried letting go of one of my many braids as she felt the wrath of Lisette's catholic-reminiscent slap to the hand.

"Will you stop playing in her hair if you're not going to help me?" For every four braids Lisette unraveled, I'd only done one. And for everyone I did, Ruby? *Well.* She was so busy admiring the style that she didn't have the heart to help take it down.

"So uptight, babe. Can I help it that I like the braids? I don't want them to go."

Lisette grabbed a handful of the loose hair from the pile we started. "Well here you go if you want it so bad." Ruby being the goofball that she was, held the tightly crimped hair up to her own strands.

"Now see, if this hair was a 6, then we'd be talking."

"Girl, go somewhere!" I swear, even when they bickered they were cute together. Ruby curled up on a chair to the left of the loveseat indulging in a yogurt she'd been nursing for the past few minutes; I couldn't wait to get all these braids out. I was so hungry, I could barely stand it.

Ruby's laughter in the room caused both of us to look in her direction. "What's so funny? I want to laugh." Lisette joked.

"Nah, just laughing at something Tim sent me. I swear we have, like, the stupidest inside jokes." At the mention of Tim's name, I perked up. Was it stupid of me to still be into him? We didn't talk much at work but when we did exchange words it was always friendly. The other day he even put his hands on my waist. I mean *sure*, he was trying to move me out of the way to look for something but that didn't take away from the desire I had for another chance of his hands on my body. Referring back to my previous question. *Yes.* It was stupid of me to still be into him. As long as I accepted that it shall not be pursued, my stupidity ~~should not~~ would not escalate. I was on top of this.

"Hey, did anyone DVR that last episode of Minority Report. I have to see what happened with my girl Ms. Vega." With the remote in hand, Ruby turned on the T.V.

"Ugh, why don't you people have Hulu or Netflix? I swear, the two of you are the only ones I know still paying for cable." She complained as she channel surfed, finally settling on an SVU marathon. That was pretty much death for me. Once I watched one episode, the chance of me walking away were slim to none.

In my lap, my phone vibrated, leaving me with more than

enough to dream about when it came to that last thought about Timothy. I abandoned my one-braid-at-a-time post to check my messages, only to discover it was Ruby who was only inches away.

Ruby: *Tim just texted me, Tell Naima hi.*

Ruby: *So hi*

Ruby: *And what's that about anyway? That's like the first time in a while he's mentioned you. Even if it was just to say hi. Hash things out?* 👀

The texts kept coming leaving me with so little time to reply to every last one of them.

Me: *No, not really. Just work with him every day. Hard not to be nice* 😛

Ruby: *I miss my two best friends being a couple. We never got a chance to double date or anything.*

Me: *You're so corny* 😊

Ruby: *He hasn't come out and said it but I think he really misses you. Since you got back he's less cranky all of a sudden. Just an observation.*

Me: *Yea, yea. Sure, sure.*

Ruby: *So pessimistic. Boo.* 👎

Even if that were true, I had a feeling we would never go there again. We were just two people that hurt each other who were both too stubborn for our own goods. #LeosvsAquariuses

It was just a thought but…I think I missed him too.

CHAPTER FIVE

Timothy

With my only day off this week, I'd planned to make better use of my time then lounging around my apartment getting wrapped up in old *Dexter* episodes and eating junk food. So far this week there'd been zero time to make a proper run to the grocery store, so all I had was cold cuts and rice noodles, neither of which I had a taste for. I had half a mind to spend this day running errands, but I wanted to enjoy it. Days off were becoming scarce, and I wanted to do something to remind me that I was still human and not a robot. *I needed to get out of this apartment.*

I sent a quick *"Shoot pool?"* text to whoever I thought wasn't busy, but all I got back was a bunch of *"No's,"* *"Why you ain't ask me earlier,"* or *"How about tomorrow's?"* I was the only one of my friends who worked almost every weekend, so I hadn't been going out lately. Thought about dropping by the job, but that was just sad. I could've gone to the gym, I wasn't in the mood to sweat.

The only thing I could think of doing myself without feeling like that creep at a bar was hitting up a movie. I hated going to the movies, but when I did go, going by myself made it easier to movie hop if I wasn't feeling the flick I'd paid for. With what was playing nearby, I had a feeling I might have to experiment.

❦

The parking at Providence Place was expensive—ten bucks just to go to the mall—but all the other theatres in the area were art house screenings, and I was in the mood for something mainstream. It was warm out, but I grabbed a baseball cap from the backseat once I did a rake through and felt it was dry. A ride to the mall did just the trick. A quick check in the mirror had me glad that I'd taken the time to shave. Laziness had me looking like a straight-up lumberjack, but not today. I felt like something amazing was supposed to happen, so it didn't hurt that I looked as good as I felt.

Navigating through the mall was the worst part. I was always tempted to hit up stores after seeing some displays in the windows of shit I know I didn't need. But if I wanted to make the movie, I'd have to trek through the mall without making unnecessary stops. *Mission completed.*

I let out a sigh of relief seeing the lobby nearly empty. *Note to self: start going to the cinema on Wednesdays.* I was claustrophobic when it came to opening weekend crowds, so the calm didn't bother me.

"Can I get one for *High Stakes*?" I asked the cashier behind the ticket counter. She had this wild display of hair color and face piercings that would actually be kind of cute if she didn't look to be in her late teens. Kind of reminded me of Kat Von D with purple hair.

"Did you want IMAX or regular?" she asked with a smile.

"Hmm… Let's go with IMAX." Because I didn't need my ear drums and was feeling adventurous today. After she handed me my ticket and pointed me in the direction of the IMAX screenings, I made haste to the concession stand and indulged in an extra-large Slurpee, as well as an overpriced box of Sweet Tarts and strawberry-flavored Twizzlers. Possibly tonight's dinner.

My eyes lit up when I noticed Ruby and Lisette walking up to the concession stand. Ruby had my absolute respect for bagging Naima's roommate. *Girl was fine*, and I was hating hard when she'd brought her to Symposium's Fourth of July cookout. I was weird in a way where I liked to see two younger women in love, holding hands, not giving a shit about what the world thought about them.

My mom was someone who was married, had kids, and divorced all by the time she was twenty-nine. After my sister passed, it took her a long time to learn how to be happy. Part of that had been coming out to the world. She became more of a person when she'd met my stepmom twelve years ago. So I always regretted not being able to see my mom young, starry-eyed for a woman she genuinely loved with feathered hair and ugly eighties prom dresses.

"Evening, ladies. Just when I think I have a day off, I run into Ruby and I feel like I'm at work," I said as I took a sip from my cherry-and-Coke-mixed Slurpee.

"Yeah, well, you could have driven to any theatre you wanted to, but your lazy ass drives here. Your fault, Timbo, your fault." Ruby reached in to give me a hug as Lisette and I exchanged a friendly hello. A few quick words back and forth, and I learned we were all here for the same movie. And here I thought I'd spend tonight alone.

"Mind if I join you? I mean, *unless it's date night.*"

"More like ladies' night. Naima's here, too," Lisette added. At the sound of her name, Naima loomed into view.

"What'd I miss?" We exchanged friendly glances, but Ruby and Lisette were too distracted with each other to notice. I was angry at myself for staring longer than I intended, but the way she looked tonight, it was hard as hell not to. She wore a white, off-the-shoulder blouse that cropped at her navel and a black, mid-length skirt that revealed one of her thighs through a very high slit. Her hair was styled straight, half-up, half-down, and her face was dolled up to perfection. She looked hot.

"Nah, Tim is seeing the same movie we're seeing. Mind if he tags along?"

If Naima was uncomfortable, she didn't show it. She only smiled and shook her pretty little head as we walked our way to theatre number six.

I was relieved when the girls took a row in the middle. I hated being in the front, especially at IMAX screenings since they were crazy loud and seemed even louder toward the front. When I thought about it, they probably weren't, but everyone knows how hard it is to convince yourself otherwise when you believed something to be true.

Ruby hit me with the okie-doke when she and Lisette took the two seats closest to the aisle, leaving me no choice but to sit next to Naima. This whole acting-like-I-didn't-give-a-shit was wearing me down, but I at least looked like I kept my feelings at bay on the outside. But what I wouldn't give for her to rest her head on my chest while I ran my fingers through her hair.

Ruby Woo: *Staten Island looks hot, right?*

I almost laughed out loud with Ruby's three-seats-away texting ass. Trying to get me to break.

Me: *No doubt*

Ruby Woo: *Y'all still beefing?*

Me: *Nah*

Ruby Woo: *Cool, cuz you know I don't like when my besties are beefing.*

Me: *Aww*

Lisette and Naima carried on a conversation in Spanish, a hanging reminder of one of the things that made me weak when it came to Naima. Her ability to grasp so many languages. Looks were nice, but intelligence kept me interested. Sad to say after months of trying, my interest in Naima was never going to go away. This was going to be a long-ass year.

Ruby Woo: *Ugh. I hate when they do that* 

Me: *Silly*

I couldn't exactly say the same.

Naima

"Real talk, movie was loud and that shit was garbage. I want my money back." Tim confessed what everyone was thinking. I don't know what the hell I'd watched for the past two hours, but it definitely hadn't been worth a fourteen-dollar price tag.

"Oh, c'mon, it wasn't that bad. The plot twist was *kind* of good. You can't tell me you saw that coming," Ruby said with her mouth full of candy.

"I most certainly saw it coming," Tim said. That much I'd figured since he'd murmured *"called it"* with his face in his hands the second the twist was revealed. I hadn't seen the twist coming, but I'd still thought it was corny.

One by one we exited our seating row and found ourselves back in the theatre's lobby. Timothy was kind enough to offer us all a ride home, and while I was uneasy, I had to get over my fear of interacting with Timothy. Clearly, he had no issues with talking to me, so now it was just me with the problem.

I hated how his smile made my stomach all fluttery or the way his walk made me want to sneak up behind him and put my arms around his waist. I hated how I couldn't act natural around him. Most of all I hated feeling *like* I couldn't act natural around him. I wanted things to be normal.

We walked through the mall to find the elevator to the mall's garage. Usually mall movie theaters had their own movie patron elevator leading to the parking lot but not this one. To top it off, the parking layout was the most confusing I'd ever seen, but Tim seemed to know his way.

If it hadn't been for the girls' talking, the trip to his car would've been painstakingly quiet. Tim and I were both preoccupied with our cell phones, probably doing nothing but otherwise too consumed to converse. Within minutes, his car was in sight, and he clicked the doors open with his programmed key.

Before I could claim the backseat, Ruby and Lisette hopped back there, leaving me to either be subject to their PDA or ride up with Timothy. I took my chances with up front when I overheard Ruby murmur some whack nickname striking an eerie resemblance to *snookums*.

Tim adjusted the rearview and turned back to look at them. "Y'all so cute."

They were and that's what made them even more sickening. I kept asking why my closest friends had to hook up. Providence couldn't have been that small.

"So where am I taking you ladies? Home?"

Ruby and Lisette looked between each other. "I mean, I wouldn't mind getting something to eat if anyone's down." Lisette said.

Timothy looked to me, and not wanting to be a party pooper, I agreed with the girls. At this time of night, the only open restaurants nearby were the crazy expensive ones, and the wait times weren't looking like a way I wanted to spend the next hour. I'd take my chances walking around Downtown.

"You guys, I'm straight. I'm going to just chill downtown or something. Call me when you're ready and I'll just meet you guys."

Ruby peered into me with her amber-colored doe eyes. "C'mon, Naima, just stay. I'm friggin' starving. Please."

"C'mon, mami, be considerate. Naima doesn't want to wait; she doesn't have to."

Great, so now best friends were about to start arguing about whether I came or stayed. Not wanting to ruin their night, I reassured them I wouldn't be far, but I knew the real reason Ruby didn't want me to leave was because she didn't want me to be alone.

"You know what, if it's cool with you, Naima, I'll roll with you. After all that junk food, I'm not really hungry, and plus I'm not trying to mess up any time y'all were planning to spend together."

Funny how that worked out. If I said no, I'd look like an asshole. If I said yes, I'd open an old wound of awkwardness. Like Tim, I wanted my buddies to have their time together. Hell, the only reason they even asked me to go was because they knew I'd just sit at home bored. *I suppose I'd take uncomfortable for five hundred, Trebek.*

"Sure."

"Cool. So, Ruby, Lisette, shoot either one of us a text or call when you're ready. And don't feel like you're rushing. We'll just be around here, chilling, waiting for your Bat-Signal, so please, get drunk on me."

Ruby sighed, knowing she put me in a tight position. She reached in to hug me and whispered how if things were getting weird to call her ASAP. Wasn't sure what she thought was going to happen. The worst of what we went through was at work. And things had gotten just a tad better.

"All right with just walking around?" he asked with a sharp eyebrow.

I nodded. Guess it was best to get this night over with.

It'd been a while since I'd explored this itty-bitty beautiful city. Despite living here for almost ten months, there were still small sectors I'd yet to uncover in downtown Providence, and I loved every minute of it when I did.

Providence was a place I'd describe for the most part as modern and historic and clean with its blend of nineteenth century mercantile buildings and occasional Victorian-styled architectural designs. We didn't talk much, and that was okay. I was too impressed with the park we stumbled into to provide any useful conversation anyways.

The area was filled with Venice-styled pedestrian bridges that made it look like a whole different place. The walkways were paved with red cobblestones, and pretty night lamps made an appearance every few feet along a waterfront. It was beautiful, particularly at night. I wondered what this place looked like in the daytime.

"Want to sit?" he said as we approached a metal park bench. I nodded. He rested his arms along the back as he kicked his foot out, shaking it back and forth. I thought it was going to be one of those quiet sit-downs, but he eased my nerves when he started talking.

"You should see this place in the summertime. They have all these shows and bonfires. All those things in the water light up when they have events here. It's dope. You'd like it." He bent down to rest his elbows on his knees, a brief silence filling the air. I was reminded of how much I was a sucker for his deep brown eyes when he fixed his gaze on me. "Hey, how was your summer by the way?"

I shook my head, dumbfounded. How could I make a few months sweeping floors at my aunt's shop and a temporary translating job at the hospital sound like a blast?

"Yeah…pretty uneventful. I actually couldn't wait to come back here. Not enough going on back home." I chewed on my nails. "What about you?"

He shrugged half-heartedly. "Eh, you know me. Just work and TV. Outside of that, no real story to tell." He laughed. "Although it does feel kind of weird to be out of school now. For so long, it was a part of my identity, and now it's like…I have a degree. How the hell did that happen?" His eyes crossed, and I couldn't help but laugh at his silliness.

"Well, I guess I'll know how you feel soon. Just a few months to go as an undergrad. Let's pray I can find a friggin' job before I go for my M.A. Which, with what my money looks like, I'm going to have to put a hold on that for a while. *Pay off some of these loans.*"

"I hear that. Soon as I get a raise, the loans be like, *what raise*? I long for the days they aren't a part of the equation. Until then…" He pulled off his baseball cap and forked his fingers through his dark hair. Even with its new shape, it was still unruly, still sexy as always and headed in several different directions.

"You want to head to my car? The girls should be getting out sooner than we know it. What have we been out here for—a half hour or so? Pretty sure if Ruby gets a few drinks in Lisette, those two aren't going to feel like walking. C'mon."

I took one last look at the waterfront and trailed behind him on the way to his car.

❧

Timothy

The hardest thing about being around Naima while we weren't at work was finding a reason to look at her. With work, it was easy. I could easily ask her a question that didn't cause suspicion. *Did you go on break yet? Could you help me out in the pantry? Do you mind if I send you to the floor?* All innocent and deemed appropriate.

The idea that I could be checking her out would never catch on. There was always a reason to look her way. Now, I knew if I did steal a glance, I wouldn't be able to stop looking. She was still one of the most beautiful women I'd ever laid eyes on. Just a few seconds too long and I knew my bottled-up feelings for her would undo me. I couldn't go out like that, not when I wasn't exactly over her, not when I was still putting the pieces of myself back together.

We sat in my car for a few silent minutes until the sound of her giggles broke the silence. I turned to her, smiling. "What?"

A vampy red lipstick stained her pout, making her smile even sexier as her kohl-rimmed eyes glowed a soft black in the dim light.

"Nothing, it's just…you have this one lick of hair that always sticks out. It has a mind of its own. It takes all the strength inside of me not to put it back in place. You know how I am with hair, Tim."

Naima was the empress of fly hairstyles. Every day she came into work with the intent to slay. Be it straight or kinky, up or down, she was the one to talk to when your hair looked a mess. For me, that was most of the time.

"Okay, so you're the expert then. Fix it," I flirted.

Up for the challenge, she leaned in and tousled her fingers along the tips of my strands and laughed. "It'd probably help if I had some sort of…you know what it is. That stuff that people with straight hair use for hold…"

"*Mousse?*" I said, trying to sound condescending.

She yanked at my hair, which brought a tinge of pain to my scalp, but reminded me of all the times she'd pulled at my tresses in dirty moments. Moments where I had her pleasure at my control. As a reaction, I kissed the inside of her forearm. She pulled away awkwardly as we sat there in a moment of silence.

"Shit. I'm sorry. I just—" Before I could explain, her lips smothered mine in a kiss. I wanted to push her away. Tell her that the need to kiss her left a long time ago when she'd shattered my heart in a million pieces. But now that she was here, I couldn't fight the feeling that laid dormant for so long inside me. I needed someone.

No. Saying *someone* implied that just anyone would do. Who I needed was *her*.

We kissed for a while before realizing something was meant to happen. The stowage and cup holders were only keeping us apart.

"There's more room in the backseat," I said, hoping she would take the bait.

Without argument, our car doors swung open as we made our way to the backseat of my Audi. I bit my lip at the sight of how hot she looked. It was still warm out for fall, but goosebumps formed where my hands rubbed her thighs. The slit in her skirt highlighted her sexy legs in a way that made me feel unworthy, but I'd be sure to earn my keep in the next few moments that passed.

She took her hair down, and it fell in dark layers along her shoulders and back. She didn't waste time initiating intimacy, one of the things I'd missed most about her. When she wanted it, she didn't always wait for me to get the ball rolling. She pulled me in closer and guided my mouth to hers.

"I don't know how your lipstick in still intact," I said as my lips trickled down to her neck. She let out a breathy moan when my fingers found their way to the inside of her panties. "Fuck, you're so wet right now. Now the only thing I can think about is tasting you," I said, my teeth biting the curve of her shoulder.

"Then do it already and stop teasing me."

Just for that, I planned on doing just that. She laid down on her back, and I pulled her skirt off and tossed it into the front seat. I kneeled in to kiss her hips that I'd missed so much, pulling down her panties inch by inch until they reached her ankles and eventually got thrown off with her skirt. My lips teased her legs until I found myself all the way down her thighs, my tongue exploring everywhere but where she pleaded me to be.

"That feels so good. I swear, I fuckin' hate it when you do that."

With the tip of my tongue, I drew a line from the bottom of

her pussy to the hood of her clit. "But you like it when I do that, right?"

That devilish look in her eye gave me my answer. My lips feathered kisses on her stomach while my hands were at work pulling down her top. She had on one of those strapless bras that took more than two hooks to strip her out of. Once I had it off, I planned on giving her breasts the attention they deserved. Her stomach caved in as my tongue swirled circles around her pert brown nipples, my fingers tracing their way to her center. She swore at the feel of my fingers inside her.

"*Mmm*, I think I want to taste you now," I said, still moving in and out of her entrance. She was so warm, so wet. I wanted to feel her get wetter.

With my free hand, I licked my fingers and spread her pretty lips open, letting the moisture from my fingers add to her slickness. My tongue was next in line to add to the fun. There was something about her taste that made me hard as shit. The way her legs squeezed around my neck as her fingers pulled at my hair made me think I could eat her pussy all day.

Her moans grew louder, and her legs began to shake at the steady glide of my fingers inside of her.

"Mmm… That's your spot there, isn't it?"

She shivered, rolling her eyes back, but managed to blurt out "yes" as her nerves went into overdrive.

"Good, because you're gonna come for me. Can you come for me, baby?" Simultaneously my tongue and hands went to work as her legs became tighter around my neck until they were tight no more.

Her breath came out in heavy pants as she let out one last cry, her legs now a limp, useless mess. My fingers were still gliding inside her. "Oh my god, Naima. You are, like, stupid wet right now."

She pulled on my shirt, bringing my mouth to hers as she

sexily tasted herself off my tongue. "So you gonna fuck me or what?" she said with a smile.

"*Fuck*, Naima. It pains me to say this but looks like we're going to have to call it a night. I'm not carrying."

She leaned up. "You're kidding right? What happened to, '*I always carry condoms on me, I'm a guy. It's not that serious.*'"

If I was being honest, it had been a while for me, so I hadn't exactly been adding condoms to my weekly grocery list. That and I wasn't eager to hook up with anyone. That is, until now.

"C'mon, I know you have to have a secret stash in here. Just look and I promise if you find none…I'll do other things."

I was really tempted to indulge in those other things, but if my dick was telling me something, it was that I wanted to fuck. I pillaged through every compartment my disappointing car had, but just as I suspected, I came up short. *Shit.*

"Yeah, it's looking like a no. Unless you're willing to take a ride really quick to get some." Just as I suggested it, both of our cell phones buzzed with notifications. I pulled my phone out my pocket.

"*Fuck*, it's Ruby." *There go those other things.* I hit the answer button. "Hey, you done? … Nah, we're just now walking to my car," I said with a grimace as I handed Naima her panties and skirt from the front seat. "No, no, no. Stay where you are. I'll be there in like five minutes. … Cool. See you then." Naima managed to get dressed in record speed, checking her hair and makeup a few times before hopping in the front seat. I drove a few blocks with the windows down, trying to disguise any hint of what had just gone down in the back seat. It didn't smell like full-on sex, but it'd be foolish to think two girls who dated girls wouldn't recognize the familiar scent of fluids on my face. That was just sloppy.

In three short blocks, Ruby and Lisette stood patiently in front of the restaurant, waiting as I pulled up.

"It's a good thing y'all skipped this place. Food was high as hell, and their burgers were dry. Like, how do you fuck up a burger? Then they try and call it gourmet," Lisette spat.

Ruby reached up into the space between us, leaning her elbows on each side. "What did you guys get into?"

"Oh, we just walked around. Waited for you. Nothing major," Naima answered, paying special attention to her phone before she laid it across her lap. Ruby followed with a few other questions but lost interest with all of Naima's less-than-exciting answers. She sat back in her seat as I took this as the time to see if Naima was open to hang out at my place. If her number was still the same, I never deleted it. I hit send before I could change my mind.

Me: *Wanna come through?*

Her phone blinked on as she reached for it, her thumbs tapping fiercely against the screen.

Naima: *So what? We can finish what we started?*

I looked to my phone and balanced it in my hand as I drove.

Me: *Don't have to do anything you don't want to do. Just wanted some company.*

"Hey, Tim. You know the light is green, right?" Ruby said, making me put my phone in my lap. I pressed my foot on the gas and took off into the road. The screen to my phone lit up, and I picked it up once again to take a peek.

"Fuck our lives, I guess," Ruby said with a whole lot of snark.

"Ruby, relax. If I wanted you all dead, trust me, it wouldn't be in my baby."

Naima: *Cool if I wait for the girls to go to sleep? Just don't want them asking me all these questions.*

Me: *After I drop y'all off, just shoot me a text when ready.*

With a few bends and turns, I pulled up to Naima and Lisette's apartment as they all said their goodbyes. It was nice hanging out with Ruby again. Since she'd started dating Lisette, we hadn't spent that much time together, but I was happy that she had a good reason to not be around. *Lisette was a very good reason to not be around.* Especially compared to me. I waited until they all went inside before shooting Naima another text message.

Me: *Heading home. The earlier, the better.*

She texted back within seconds.

Naima: *Will see what I can do...*

CHAPTER SIX

Naima

Why was it the only time Ruby and Lisette wanted to have some late-night girl time was when I was waiting for them to take their asses in the room so I could call Tim to come get me? It was a random act on both our parts, totally drunk off the moment and fast-paced, even for us. Was it *just* hooking up? Was I reading too much into it? How he made me feel tonight was just what I needed to get me out of my seven-month dry spell but… Was I setting myself up to get hurt again by wanting something more?

Tim: *Status?*

Me: *Still up…*

Tim: *Still? Any chance they'll be asleep by midnight? That's about when I fall asleep these days.*

I looked at the time. 11:17. Fuck. These chicks were getting on my nerves.

"You guys, I think I'm going to take a shower and hit it for the day. I have a test in the morning. You know how it is."

Lisette didn't need any more convincing, but Ruby was

bummed out that she couldn't get anything useful out of me about my time spent with Tim.

"Can I just grab some things from my dresser?"

"Naima, you're good. Haven't you had enough of that couch? Plus, I'm tired. I'm not even trying to do anything." Ruby rolled her eyes in a familiar way I knew too well. Poor girl. I rummaged through my dresser and grabbed a white lace demi bra and its matching set of V-strings. I loved the way white popped against my skin tone, and if I wanted to feel like a temptress, this was the way to do it. To get it past the girls with no probing, I wrapped it in a baggy heather-red T-shirt and a pair of grey yoga pants and whisked off to the shower.

Four minutes shy of twelve, I sent Timothy a quick text to see if he was still up. His reply was in seconds.

Me: *Is it too late?*

Tim: *Nope. OMW.*

Within fifteen minutes, he pulled up in front of the house in his Audi A6. His normally deafening music was cut low on a mellow R&B station. We took one look at each other, unable to hold back our laughter. He was wearing a dark red shirt and light grey sweatpants, almost identical to my look.

"And they said bum chic wouldn't make a comeback. Really, though, we have to fire our stylists. I'm thinking I was rockin' some exclusive shit," he joked. "Need to stop anywhere before we head to my place?"

I shook my head, wanting to be clear into the roads right now just in case one of the girls woke up and worried. It's not like I hadn't planned on telling them, but right now there was nothing to tell.

On the way to his house, he took an alternate turn to his usual route. "Did I tell you I moved?" *That explained it.* Turns out he'd moved downtown in a place that was literally footsteps away from the mall and, as a brief observation, a lot fancier. While his last place hadn't been all that bad, this apartment complex was a huge step up. It had everything from a twenty-four-hour gym to a clubhouse where residents could host parties. Hell, the place even had a concierge, a swimming pool, and a damn movie theatre. Tell me why he'd leave this place?

Where his former apartment was sleek and muted, this one had new furniture, a new concept, and almost twice as much room. "Wow, I like what you've done with the place."

He laughed. "I wish I could take all the credit but sixty-percent of this stuff my moms picked out and purchased. Called it a graduation gift."

Damn, I wish my folks would hook me up like that. The most I ever got was from my step-dad because Nigerian parents would never dream of spoiling their children. He slipped off his sandals and walked over to his sofa to turn on the TV.

"I know it's late, but I'm wide awake now. Want to watch something?"

His place was new to me, but it was still weird to be back here again. In his personal space. I'd spent months wondering how he was doing, if he ever thought of me, and if we'd ever get back to where we were. *If you even wanted to call this where we were.* He laid across the couch, draping himself in an oversized comforter. It wasn't until he called out to me that I realized I was standing there, lost in a daze.

"You don't have to stand there looking like a lost animal." He gestured for me to join, so join him I did. I'm not sure if I thought this moment would be different or if I wanted it to be different, but it was nice resting my head on his chest. "Comfy?" he asked as he flipped through the channels. He spent five minutes flipping through channels he'd never watch before settling on *The Office* with Steve Carell.

"Ever watch this show? It's one of those sleeper funny shows.

You have to really watch it and commit to it to uncover its charm. Full disclosure, I like it," he added in a sleepy voice.

His hands traveled up my shirt and disappointingly rested on my stomach. Feeling his palm on my skin sent urges to that area that hadn't stopped thinking about what had occurred between us just a few hours ago. I know I could have sat here and just enjoyed the comfort of lying here, being cozy and being close, but it wasn't close enough. I longed to fuel that spark we once had.

I wiggled around to face him, his eyes closed as his chest rose and lowered. Poor thing was asleep. He looked so peaceful when he slept, all sweet and precious and unknowing of all the ongoing stress that plagued us in our everyday lives. Looks had never been important to me, but it was vexing how attractive I found Timothy. His semi-full lips, his masculine chin, even the way his dark features contrasted with his fair skin all made him remarkably handsome. But so was his mind—you got lost in his interests, his thoughts, the way he looked at the world. *Why was he so damn perfect to me?*

I sat up, watching him instinctively adjust himself as I lifted up his shirt. Damn, I missed this body. He was the right amount of lean and sculpt without being too bulky, and while he wasn't big on tatts (I know, I know—a rarity these days), the few he had were placed proper in a way that didn't take away from the perfection he called a torso. My lips settled on the curve of his neck, getting drunk off the herbal scent of his shampoo and the clean fresh scent of his skin. He rustled in his spot as my mouth reached his ear. He gave me a lopsided grin, his hands loosely gripping my waist.

"*Mmm*…sleepy," he said without opening his eyes as I snaked down to his thick, hard ridge. He didn't fight me slipping him out of his pants. Sleepy, my ass.

He twitched the moment my tongue dipped into the trail of his V-line, his swollen cock rising to the occasion. Maybe I was alone on this one, but there was something amazingly empowering about being able to please a man in more ways than one. That wasn't to say I preferred giving head over having sex, but the way someone could make you feel like no one in the world did it quite like you did was reason enough to make it one of my go-tos. Plus, I loved pleasing the one I cared about. No shame in my talents for someone who so selflessly took care of you in the same way.

He bit his lip as the sight of my tongue traveling in tormentingly slow licks from base to tip, the look of longing reading clear on his sexy expression. Hunger beckoned me to take him all in one try, and I did, over and over, until he gathered my hair in his fist, willing me to go at his pace.

My hands and lips worked in unison as they twisted up and down his cock. A groan escaped his lips just moments after I switched up my speed.

"Yeah, I'm gonna have to stop you right there. That shit feels good, but what I really want is for you to fuck me."

No arguments there. He'd said the magic words.

There was a wrestle to his room, one that left piles of clothes on the floor in its wake. It wasn't long before we were sprawled across Timothy's mattress, body to body. Skin to skin. I could tell that he wanted this, but his light short breaths betrayed his wired state. I was going to have to give him a reason to stay awake.

"Mmm… You feel so good right now," he said, dragging his fingers alongside the back of my thighs. He pulled me closer, to the point I didn't think we could fit any closer without him actually being inside me. He moved around, but as I crawled on top, I reached over his head to pin down his arms.

Flirtatious laughter filled the quiet space, leaving any awkward stigma in the living room. I wish I could say things felt weird, but in this moment they just…*didn't*. Maybe the moment after the fact would be. Maybe neither of us would be concerned with any awkwardness. *Right now?* If the night could mirror everything about this moment, we'd have nothing to worry about.

He fought to lean up, but I was quick to pin him right back on the bed. "I always did like when you were bossy," he laughed, biting his lower lip. He pretended to stay pinned to the mattress, but gestured toward his dresser. "Before I forget. Made a pit stop. Top shelf, right dresser."

It took me out of the game for a few seconds to reach for the unopened box of condoms in the drawer. I'd only left my post a moment before I felt Tim lean in and graze his teeth against my backside. I couldn't help but tremble at how good it felt. How much I'd missed it like crazy when he teased me like that. It was best to have them as close as possible. Never knew how soon things happened. I ripped the box open with urgency, leaving one near the pillow next to his head. I was ready to blow off some tension, and there was no better time than now.

It was never a music-filled, rose-petal-to-the-room type moment, but Tim and I always knew how to have fun. I couldn't even think of a better time we had, that hadn't been spontaneous or far from put-together. It made everything boiling down to the point feel that more explosive, and I wouldn't want it any other way.

Traces of his stubble tickled my neck as his lips pressed alongside the column of my throat. Short tingles warmed the spot of contact, curling my toes as he ran his teeth lightly against the skin of my neck. He was in no rush to get to my lips, his mouth making its way toward my neck, chin, and jawbone. It didn't take more than a few strategic movements for Tim to slip the condom on. I took my sweet time lowering onto his cock, watching his chest rise and fall as I took him.

A low groan escaped his throat, his hands gently exploring the visible mounds of my body. Someone's touch shouldn't have that much effect on your sanity, but the state of mine melted away at every covered inch. My defenses deteriorated at each inch my body rode his delectable length. As if that weren't enough, his thighs met every earth-shattering stroke, each thrust perfectly in sync with my swiveling hips.

All my sensitivity went into overdrive as Tim's tongue graced my nipples, sending warm sensations where he devoured them, cold and tingly sensations where he blew.

"I've been dying to do this again for so long," Tim said under his breath. I could barely register what he said, under the sound of his skin slapping against mine, mixed in with the wordless music we made together. The sound of his voice broke as my body clenched tighter against him.

"Damn, girl. I'm about to come. Are you close?"

"No, but it's okay," I said, slowing my rhythm. "You had me earlier. Much appreciated, too."

Timothy growled and slapped his hands alongside my behind. I shouldn't have liked it so much, but it just added to the fun. He bit down on his lip, grabbing hold of my hips. It was too bad I wasn't close. My body was too on board not to be. But this wasn't just to rock my socks off—I wanted to connect. Most of all, I wanted to connect to him.

Timothy took control of the speed as I held on tight to his shoulders. His face distorted in a number of unreadable expressions that he might otherwise not have wanted me to see. But without killing the moment, he looked cute. If by cute, you mean hilarious at the same time.

"You sure it's okay if I come?"

"You must not want to if you keep asking me."

Timothy laughed off my comment, continuing on with his current rhythm. Three powerful thrusts did him in, and he held onto me with each throbbing pulse. I leaned in to kiss him as he tried to catch his breath, wiping thin films of sweat from his forehead. There wasn't much to do but roll off. He threw his head back on the pillow.

"Aw, man, Naima. That was..." he started, drawing out one

last breath. "I needed that. You don't know how much I needed that. You don't need me to drop you off at home, do you?"

As easier as it would be to go back now and not have to explain where I was and who I was with to the girls, I was in no rush to go home to an empty couch. I shook my head.

"Good because I would have spent the next half-hour talking you out of it. I don't feel like doing shit right now." He forked his fingers through his damp strands and scooted downward to lay his chin on my stomach. "Plus, the half-hour I would have wasted convincing you is a half-hour I could have spent getting you off. I'm not going to be able to sleep knowing you didn't get there. "

"And how do you know I didn't sneak one on you?"

He snickered. "*Seriously?*" He pressed his lips just a few inches above my navel, a flood of sensations coursing through me.

"Well, for one, you still have nerves left where there should be none. And second, you do this thing with your voice. Like a growling sound. It's kind of cute. Plus, Naima, it hasn't been that long." *If you didn't consider seven months a long time.*

He continued kissing my stomach, but the moment he went below the navel, I yanked him by the hair.

"Oww."

"Can I take a shower first?"

His lips pressed into a hard line as he rested on his elbows. "It's just me."

That much was true, but I was paranoid about enjoying myself if I didn't feel at my best. This was no surprise. He minutely shook his head and gestured to the hallway.

"Feel free to take a shower, but if that's the case, I'm coming with. Any objections?"

❀

Timothy

Whoever thought of showering with a person as an alluring act clearly never showered with a woman. It was supposed to be sexy, but the time it took for a woman to complete the simplest task, such as washing her face, was so *not* sexy. Four steps was a whole lot of legwork for something that only took me three seconds to do with soap and water. But Naima had a system. A system that would soon leave us in cold water.

"Look, um…I'm not trying to rush you, but we need to switch it up or something."

Her jaw clenched before she sighed out loud. How dramatic. But cute. Thankfully she was open to swap.

"I'm about to show you how to take a shower in five minutes or less."

I turned my back to her, letting the warm water saturate my skin and hair as the steam enhanced my sense of smell. Naima's fingertips grazed the sides of my ribcage, the soapy trace of her touch washing away with the water.

"You know I've never asked you what your tattoos meant."

Instinctively, I lifted up my arm to the one in question.

"You tell me, Ms. Modern Languages."

She sucked her teeth. "Well, it looks Latin. For your information, I've never taken an interest in Latin."

"Ah, then it's the perfect lesson for you. Repeat after me: *Discere Faciendo*."

Or in other words, learn by doing. She repeated the words back in a more convincing accent than I could ever muster up. "So what about the other one?"

II.II.MCMXC-V.XIX.MCMXCV

My sister's birthdate and date of death in Roman numerals. That one was actually my first tattoo. I figured if I was going to get them, they might as well mean something to me.

"Hey, Tim?"

"Yeah?"

"Do you feel as if anything's wrong with this situation?"

I knew it was coming, just not when to expect it. Our fallout from winter. A subject I really didn't want to talk about, happily avoided, and just wanted to put behind me.

"Maybe I'm just overthinking, but it feels like we've gone from there to here in less than a day. As awesome as that is, I feel like I'm in a dream or something. Like, I'll wake up any minute and we'll be back to square one. I want to be friends and I don't know…say more than three words to each other."

"Don't you think it's a little late for that?" I joked.

"Tim, I'm serious."

"Okay, so here's the deal. The past is the past. I don't see the point in talking about something that happened months ago. Especially when it appears both of us has moved on from that point. Agreed?"

She bit her lip, exhaling deeply. She nodded once.

"Now, as much as I would love to stay here and watch you lather up that beautiful body of yours, I am finito and want to shave." I pulled the curtain back and stepped out onto the floor mat, securing a towel around my hips.

My skin tingled at the application of shaving cream I so generously applied to my face. Having dark hair and pale skin made my five-o'clock shadow look like it grew in overnight. Stubble wasn't so bad the first day, but knowing Naima, she'd probably complain about the rest. Off that went.

"See you in the room," I said to her as I made my way back to my quarters. I slipped into some clean boxers and laid down on my bed, looking to waste time until Naima joined me.

Were we okay? Of course we were okay. Here we were—two people who'd spent the last six months avoiding each other, now sleeping together like nothing had even happened. Why couldn't we focus on that? Why was it so important to dive into what *had* happened versus the present moment in time?

Even though I wasn't trying to avoid the conversation, I didn't want to have it now. Granted, with our track record? It was completely justified to have some doubts or second thoughts. I know I didn't have the answer to every question or problem. I didn't expect her to either. But things were different now.

The same obstacles didn't stand in our way. Not to say there was no margin of error at all, but based on our past, one could only go up from there.

A light sigh escaped my throat as I thought about the year before. Those months had been some of my best, but at the risk of being some of the lowest points in my life, too. I hadn't known you could feel *that* bad and good at the same time. But I refused to dwell on it anymore. No one would forget those times, but the best we could do was make up for old ones.

Naima slipped back into bed before I could process the moment. "Tired?" I said, rubbing the temples of my forehead.

Naima giggled, hiding herself under the covers. "Tell me about it."

I soon followed suit. It was easy not to think about anything when you sunk into the curve of the mattress. Only this time, it was accompanied by the curve of her. I couldn't believe I'd almost forgotten what it felt like to be here like this. I kissed her on the lips. "Goodnight."

"Night."

I reached over to flick off the light and finally turned in.

CHAPTER SEVEN

Timothy

Sometimes I wasn't sure taking on Ravinder's responsibilities was worth the new stress. The job itself *looked* easy. Ravinder definitely made it appear that way. But the art of visual merchandising was much harder than it looked. There was so much to the position people didn't see, and it was all to maximize sales.

Studying floor plans and POS displays wasn't an easy task. Last month's back-to-school display even had me wanting to go for an extra semester, just so I could impulse-buy some of those overpriced textbooks.

I trained with him nearly half the week. *Why didn't my shit look like his?*

Maybe it was too similar to decorating, something I'd never had a strong eye for in the first place. Or a little like buy-this-on-impulse *Tetris*. The more appealing it was to the eye, the more a customer would stop to look. Maybe even consider a purchase. It'd probably take more than a few months to have the eye for detail Ravinder had twelve years to have.

I could tell you what looked good with certain outfits. I was even a decent judge on which spices complimented which meals best. Hell, if a zombie apocalypse started that afternoon, I had six different ways I could make it back home, even if the place was swarmed.

Now that was skill.

My first attempt at this floor plan? Couldn't say "don't quit your day job." In a few weeks, this *would* be my day job. At least Ravinder was good at raising my morale. He claimed I'd get better as time went, especially since I'd been so good at holding down the cafe. Looked like it'd take time to gain that same confidence on the sales floor.

Maybe a little trial and error? I'd probably fail at this job before I got better. And I'd only get better if I failed, just to see what worked. I had one advantage. It was so close to my favorite holiday, I was amped to make things work.

Halloween and Timothy went together like PB&J. I was looking forward to October so much that, even though I had Symposium's typical displays, I was willing to hit up an arts and crafts store and buy things out of pocket. The least I could do was put my best foot forward *first,* not last. I was taking the lead, so I didn't want to let anyone down.

As if I didn't have enough to worry about, I was also in charge of organizing the off-site event at WaterFront Park this year. Symposium usually participated in one way or another. The past few years we'd been sponsors, but this year we were hosting our own booth. I actually couldn't wait to for it, considering it was the first suggestion of mine that Ravinder actually greenlit. We always hosted local authors, but in prep for Halloween, we reached out to writers who wrote horror and paranormal. Even some romance authors, which I expected to raise participation amongst women.

What was I worried about? *I had this.*

Now if only the rest of my life navigated as easily as a floor plan. Even though work was ever-changing, overwhelming to the point I feared I'd never get the hang of things, it was *still* easier than my personal life.

Every time something felt right, I'd think back to February, when everything went wrong, and I'd just shut down. Seemed like things were always meant to go to shit.

Don't get me wrong. I liked that me and Naima were cool again. In fact, *I really liked it.* But was I ready for this bomb? I already had so much on my plate. I wanted to be all-in to get this job down before switching over, but I had human needs. I didn't want to use Naima, but I wasn't sure I could handle more than sex.

We talked, but never a serious conversation. I didn't even know whether I could handle one at this point that wouldn't make me remember the things we'd both lost.

Breaking up with my ex had been scary. It'd be cruel to say it hadn't taken a small piece of me. It was four years. But *that* part of me that'd missed her didn't miss her anymore. To be honest, it stopped a long time ago. It'd felt free as hell to come back without my baggage, a dark cloud and the weight of so much guilt weighing me down. It wasn't right what I did to her. It'd never been right.

But I thought I'd come back with me and Naima beating the odds. Only to be left twice as heartbroken. Real talk, I fucking deserved it. There were a dozen other ways I could've handled last year that wouldn't have resulted in my right now. But a dozen other ways wasn't reality. Reality ended up like this. Whatever *this* was.

It wasn't that frequent. Not like before. Maybe our never-ending schedules were to blame. Her class schedule, not to mention my twelve- to fourteen-hour days didn't make it easy. In the time she'd been back, we'd hooked up three times tops. But maybe that was good for us. It meant we didn't have to overthink things. I wanted to feel good, not think. Even the short times with Naima...

Felt damn good.

✿

Naima

Where did all those people come from? Now I admit, Symposium rushes weren't nearly as bad as a chain coffee shop. But for no book club event or holiday, Ruby and I were on edge for the last thirty minutes, and neither of us could explain the traffic. Maybe because she bounced everywhere, I hadn't known she was actually head barista. It explained why she knew her ends and outs like Timothy, but she cross-trained so many positions in the store, I was convinced she friggin' lived here.

Tim was leaving the cafe in a few weeks, and I wondered who they'd get to replace him. Would they hire in? Hire out? Hopefully it'd be some old guy sans the floppy hair and hundred-watt smile. Not that I couldn't keep my eye on the prize, but we didn't need two Timothys around here.

We'd let our…*whatever* it was get weird.

Were we having sex or not? Last time I checked, we were. But in the weeks we'd managed to, it wasn't nearly as frequent as before. Not that I needed it, but shit. A girl's got itches to scratch, too.

I didn't know if I was seeing things or whether it was on purpose, but Tim was much more professional around me since I got back. We were at work, so I got it. Perhaps he'd always just been too casual to be a manager to begin with. I'm sure the position he was training for required a lot more professionalism than over here. Yup, that sounded better than just wanting people not to catch on about us.

I didn't expect a parade. I just didn't know what we were. It felt like too much hope for a bleak situation. I couldn't ignore what had happened months prior. It had been painful and messy, and the fact we were even here seemed like progress. But if I was going avoid another last year, I needed to know what we were.

I could ask and just *know* or continue to play the patience game. But neither option worked for me. I was as patient as a starving person in a McDonald's drive-thru and sheepish as hell to avoid getting egg on my face.

I wanted to be in control this time.

First step: pretend not to notice Tim approaching the cafe counter. We were out of cupcakes—what better time to snatch some from the freezer?

"Hey, Staten Island, you get a chance to choose your next book of the month? Was discussing floor plans and wanted to get a head start on the visual layout for November."

That's right. I was the Customers' Favorite. With my hectic school schedule, my free time spent at work, plus adding in my Tim situation, the last thing I'd been worried about was picking out some book.

"Um, there's this one YA book online that looked interesting. *Black Beauty* by Constance Burris or something like that?" It had been out for a little while but my last weekend back home I'd seen it in my twelve year old niece's hands. I had no idea what the book was even about but spurted out the first book that came to my head. *Smooth.*

Tim tapped the counter from the other side, satisfied with my answer.

"Cool. I don't think we have that one stocked, so I may have to order it."

Since it'd slowed down, Ruby finally had time to restock the bins, and she materialized from the double doors separating the store from the pantry.

"Hey, Sailor Moon, got that financial report I asked for?"

Ruby slammed the two boxes of coffee grounds on the counter, sliding the folders underneath to Timothy's hands. He sorted them with a flick and pulled them up to his face. "Thanks."

Ruby shooed him away, taking the boxes and placing them on the floor where they wouldn't clutter the front as she used her box cutter to open and sort the contents inside. Tim stood there, like he was waiting for someone to say something to him. Maybe it was because they'd known each other so long, but just knowing he was standing there, apparently made Ruby more aggravated.

Wasn't I meaning to fetch those cupcakes? A little time passing in between wouldn't look like I was nervous. If he sat there another minute, it wouldn't look rude to excuse myself. I'd just look like I'm working.

"So, ladies. We're looking for volunteers to work the Halloween festival. Any takers?"

Ruby laughed out loud, so it was obvious what her answer was. I didn't think Symposium attended any such-called festivals, so I followed up.

"Is it at the store?"

"No, it's at Waterfront. Everyone's invited to be as ghouly and as gross as possible. But a Wonder Woman costume would work, too."

I'm not sure how I interested I looked. I gave him a side-eye after all. "I don't know. I was looking forward to the events around here." Granted, it sounded fun. I just didn't know enough about it to give a definite answer. "If you ask me now, I think I'm going to pass."

Ruby disappeared back beyond the doors, leaving me to fend for myself again.

"Sure you don't want to join in? It won't be big, but I think it'd be a lot of fun. I was hoping you'd say yes. Outside of the authors, it'd just be the two of us. Thought it'd give us a chance to hang out since we're busier than usual these days."

No, that didn't add any pressure. Should I be glad he wanted to hang out? It'd prove we didn't have to be intimate just to be around each other outside these doors. Plus, the approach wasn't too vague or aggressive. That was a decent sign, right? But I should stand by my original answer. No.

"Sure. Sounds fun."

Okay, that hadn't come out as planned. His eyes glistened, the light making them look more brown than black.

"You sure? Because you don't sound sure. You know you don't have to say yes just because I've asked twice. Just wanted you to know what to expect."

I was coming to the conclusion to never expect anything when it came to Timothy. "I'm sure. You can count on me."

Timothy

By the time I got down to WaterFront, most the panel tents were set up and ready. Symposium Books had a booth just between a speculative fiction and a romance books tent, so it shouldn't surprise me to have a bunch of paranormal romance sales in the near future. Definitely the right place for the in-between readers. Setting up was by no means a breeze, especially since this seemed something Ravinder would have more experience in. I'd only volunteered to show how much a team player I could be.

If Naima kept her word, she'd be here at nine. The first panel down the end didn't start until a little before ten, and I needed a second hand to mine the field. I was anxious, though. She and a *sea-bee* volunteered, both for three-and-a-half blocks. That meant we'd have a few hours to talk off and on, when I wasn't busy tending to other tasks.

Not exactly alone time, but the first time in a while we just got to chill. Nothing more. I looked forward to that. Couldn't say I hadn't missed times like that.

But in the meantime, I was getting off on the fact every person walking by wanted a double-take on my face. The outfit was my usual attire, so it was more "recently deceased" than "longtime zombie." I wasn't about to rip up my good clothes for a damn costume. But I was down to the nine of amateur face paint, along with a peel-able gash on my forehead and bite mark on my cheek. Thank you, YouTube. *Face Off* didn't have anything on me.

Maybe I could've gone a little less method, but if I was going to be here all day, might as well be the entertainment as much as the entertainment.

Why hadn't Martha opted for a payment card reader? Or at least something functional, like PayPal? Anything other than this dinosaur register I was forced to work. I'd have to be extra careful with it, especially since I only had one key to operate it with. We didn't expect to make a ton of bank, but just in case, I made sure to count our three-hundred-dollar draw as many times as it'd come up the same. Let's hope the rest of today wasn't this boring.

When a tap came at my shoulder midway into sorting a box of books, my flinched reaction caught the visitor off-guard.

"Holy shit," she said, followed by a curled upper lip and an expression of disgust.

I hoped by the time Naima arrived, I'd look terrifying enough to garner a scream. She must've known me well enough by now to expect something like this. Guess any reaction was better than no reaction. I took her outfit up and down, trying to figure out who she was.

"Hmm… You're either a gender bent Superman or—"

"I'm Supergirl, stupid."

I held up my hands in a don't-shoot-the-messenger type of way. "Just guessing. Just saw an S on your chest. Didn't want to assume." I guess if she would've been Superman, she would've been wearing pants. Either option had its benefits. Mini-skirt or tight pants. Couldn't decide what would've been sexier. I didn't know if it was the new design of Supergirl's costume, but it looked more Sailor Scout than DC Comics. I wasn't hating on being able to gawk at her in those red, knee-high boots, though.

"Wonder Woman wasn't available?"

"Boy, do you know how hard it is to find a Wonder Woman costume this time of year that doesn't fit like a swimsuit? I wanted to be comfortable. Sometimes you have to be content with just being *super*." She grabbed the stack of books in my hand, strategically placing a few on the bookshelf.

"You rocking those red boots, though." That somehow managed to escape the back of my throat in a mumble. When she asked if I'd said anything, I just chalked it up to talking to myself, which wasn't uncommon for me.

"Where do I start first?"

"Mind holding the fort at the register?"

Naima tossed a book back and forth in her hand, pouting her lower lip. "So I'm basically doing the same thing I'd be doing at Symposium?"

It took a second to explain that Symposium's panel required the attention of an organizer, so she didn't seem too disappointed after that. I'd only be gone about twenty minutes from the time the panel started and ended, and after that, it'd be smooth sailing.

She made herself comfortable on a fold-out chair behind the table. "Are we just selling books from the event?"

"That and some books from authors at the festival who weren't able to spring up for their own booth. Which reminds me, if any of them come looking to take home their books or to see how much they sold, the consignment contracts are to the left, near where my seat is."

Naima ducked underneath the table, popping her head back up only when she'd found them.

I had about ten minutes before and after to set up the panel for my guests. Thank goodness it consisted of simple tasks. The head organizer hosted the major responsibilities. I just had to make sure our guests had water, their name lanyards and tabletop name plates, and working mics. You know, *housekeeping*.

I was back before Naima got an inquiring bystander. "Looking forward to hearing anyone speak?"

She burst out laughing, bringing both hands to cover her face. "I'm sorry. It's just so hard to take you seriously with those white-out contacts. It's bad enough all the ew. I know it's the costume, but it's creepy."

To be honest, I'd forgotten I was even wearing them. They weren't always as easy to see with, but it added to the whole *undead* look. Otherwise I was just a dude with an injury.

"I'm tempted to keep them in, just to bug you. But I can't sit here for three hours and not have a real conversation, you win." I reached into my pocket to grab the contact case. They were mesh, so they came out easier, but they formed to my eye, so they wouldn't pop out.

"You're going to mess up your makeup." Naima reached over and, with a gentle hand, squeezed the outside of my lids to pop the bad boys out.

"Better?"

She shot me a sly side-eye. That curled upper lip didn't help. "Guess it'll have to do."

"You never answered my question."

"What question?" I know she hadn't forgotten that easily.

"Whether you're looking forward to anyone on the panel," I said, poking her in the shoulder.

Naima slushed through the program, eyeing every event and name on the list until the time she was out of here.

"This author sounds interesting," she said, pointing out the only author we'd never carried in the store at one point. "I think they're independently published, so I had to go online to look them up. Pretty professional-looking. Plus, it incorporated Caribbean folklore, which you *never* see in horror."

I wasn't about to brag, but I'd read a decent amount of contemporary horror books by authors of Caribbean descent. I still preferred non-fiction, but sometimes you needed a fix when the next season of your favorite show ended for the mid-season. No lie, I even liked *The Jumbies*. And it was meant for twelve-year-olds.

"Sounds cool. Every time we host an author, I do my best to get them to sign a book for me, even if it's not my taste. I can't write for shit, so I imagine how hard it must be to never reach JK Rowling success. If I can make just one author feel confident enough to start book two, why not?"

Naima rolled her eyes at that, leaning her elbows on the table. "You're so corny."

"Why? Because I'm phony?"

"No." She traced shapes along the table with her fingers. "Just that you even care enough to make somebody's day."

Hey, it made my day more than anyone else's. By that, it was worth it. I wish there was something I liked doing as much as writing for a career path.

We managed to talk up a wandering straggler browsing around our booth. While it wasn't the first time they'd been to WaterFront, it was their first time for a book-related event. Boy, were they chatty. For someone not interested in buying anything, they chatted us up for ten minutes.

Not exactly the alone time I'd hoped for, but at least it killed some time. I even told Naima I'd guard the post while she sat in for the Q&A of the horror panel. She'd have to fill me in on the details when she came back. And that wouldn't be until after I'd reset everything for the next panel.

She came back, reminding me the panel ended in two minutes, so I wasted no time heading next door. Lots of small talk, a little housekeeping, a lot of thanking people—authors and major organizers included. I couldn't imagine what they had in store for them. Some authors had more than one panel, and the other organizers had way more to do than just my minute responsibilities.

The festival didn't end until four, but Naima was only here until one o'clock. I hightailed it back over to catch Naima walking around, stretching her legs.

"Having fun?" she asked, now stretching her back.

"It's all right. Was the Q&A worth it?"

Her arms hung limply to her sides, and she skipped back to her seat. "It was all right. Wish it would've been longer." She patted her stomach for emphasis. "You don't mind if I sneak to get a snack do you?"

"No, go ahead."

More of the time we had was cut into pieces. The upside? Watching her walk away in that mini-skirt and knee-high boots. If I would've been thinking straight, I would've realized how hungry I was my damn self. Too busy indulging in another hunger. Closed mouths didn't get fed. I should've asked her to get me something. When she actually did come back, I was forced to watch her lick sugar off her lips, smacking on the churros she'd scooped up from a Mexican food vendor.

"I'm sure everyone is wondering," she said, "but since I happen to work in this department, I'm even more curious."

"Curious to what?"

"Who'll be replacing you in the cafe?"

Well played. Butter me up with the smell of churros and the sight of a mini-skirt, and folks think I'll spill the beans for anything.

"So that's what this is about?"

"Is what about?"

"You being on the sly. Scooping out, making nice talk. Probably gonna offer me a churro, too." Maybe I was getting ahead of myself. She most certainly had *not* offered me that last churro she was just now finishing.

"What they hell are you talking about?"

"You're trying to find out who your new boss will be."

"*Damn, is it a secret?*"

It wasn't something I was supposed to reveal just for the sake of it. We both knew the person. I just didn't know how unprofessional I'd look if word got around I'd told someone.

"All I can say is you've worked around them. That's all I'll say."

"Can I guess it?"

Technically that was cheating, but it did mean I didn't have to feel guilty that I was spreading confidential information. "I mean, you can. Doesn't mean I'll confirm anything."

Her eyebrow cocked as she leaned across the table to study my face. "Is it Ruby?" Damn, I should've planned a poker face. I'm sure any reaction would've given me away, but it didn't help when my lips thinned into a straight line. "I knew it!"

"I didn't confirm or deny anything. But…if I had? I'd say she's definitely earned it." Ruby started at Symposium months after me, but in that amount of time, she'd been cross-trained in multiple departments, as any future manager should. Since she was always there, her chance at a social life was shot, so I couldn't think of a better person to pass the torch to.

"You know she wouldn't tell me either? But both of your reactions were answer enough. I'm satisfied."

"I'm glad your mission at being nosy has finally been fulfilled."

She finished wiping remnants of cinnamon from her fingers. I hope it tasted as good as it looked, considering she hadn't offered any. Seemed like it gave her mega-energy, too. Somehow she talked a passerby into making the biggest purchase of the day so far—a backlist of two whole books.

"I wonder how the store's doing. I know this morning was, like, some scavenger hunt for kids or something."

"Think you're missing out?"

Naima shrugged, making herself comfortable next to me again. "No."

"Jealous, then?"

"No!" she said with extra pep. "This place is… I don't know. Cool? Wish the purchase turnout was better. Actually give me something to do. But at least the view is amazing." She pointed out the docks behind us.

"I'm just glad I'm getting paid. Fresh air. Crowds of interesting people. Somebody to talk to. What more can a man ask for?" Maybe a time machine to ask for one of those damn churros before her selfish ass ate them all, but the past was the past.

"Any plans after this?"

"What you mean, like, after the weekend?"

"I guess."

I was stuck here on a Saturday, and I worked a double tomorrow, cross-training on the floor and the cafe. The next day I'd see freedom was Monday, and that was Halloween.

"Why? Did you have plans?"

"No. That's why I was looking to make some," she said with a big smile, but it soured after my lack of reply. "Unless you're busy."

"Actually, I am." Maybe I could've articulated that better. Or thought better about my reply. I didn't know how she'd interpret four simple words, but judging by the small bout of silence, she took it the wrong way.

"Guess that shit's code for girl plans."

I laughed to myself. I was about to crack up so hard in a minute. "You're right. I do have girl plans. With an eight-year-old." Mic dropped.

"Oh."

"People still take kids trick-or-treating, you know." Rick and Brook were getting me back for that silly string incident. They were about to make me pay for having a flexible schedule. Did I think it'd be fun wasting my night going door-to-door asking people for candy? Who was I kidding? That sounded fun as hell. But since Rick and Brook's mother worked unreliable schedules and the only way a grown man could get free candy out of people was to have a kid around, it only took three or four times of me declining before I said yes.

"Well, tell Brooklyn I said hi."

"I'm just going to ignore the venom I heard just a minute ago."

"Venom?"

"Yes, venom. I hope you don't see me as that kind of dog. I'm not making an excuse. I just said I would, and I keep my word. I've only kicked it with you in these past few weeks. Trust me, juggling two people is not my idea of fun." After a tortuous last year, I couldn't do that again.

"Damn, now you're getting all personal."

"Well, it needed to be known."

"Timothy, I just asked if you had plans. I find out you do. Not a big deal."

"Well, you don't have to worry about someone else because there is no one else. I meant it when I said last year is behind us."

Naima shuffled around uncomfortably in her chair before having the courage to meet my eyes again.

"Why don't you come?"

"No, that's alright. Spend that time with your goddaughter."

"You know she likes you right?" I added, adjusting in my chair. "You wouldn't be intruding or anything."

"Tim, I said it's fine."

"We could always hang out afterwards. Or tonight if you're up to it. I'm here until nine, but I don't mind swinging by." At the suggestion her face crinkled.

"I don't know, Tim. I was sort of thinking that I'd love to see the outside of your apartment. You know, in *broad daylight.*" Not an issue at all, although, we did have a lot of fun at my apartment.

"Okay, so if I switch some things around. Take her Sunday, want to spend Monday doing something. I know you have some A.M. classes but we can start as early as you can. End late. Does that work?" She considered my idea.

"How about I grab some notes from a girl in my class and we start *extra* early."

"The plot thickens, but sounds good." And that just left how we'd planned to spend this time. Naima was usually great at expressing things that interested her so while ideas popped into my head at something new to do, I thought it best that it should be her decision since it was her suggestion.

"So Ms. Staten Island. Where is it you would like for me to take you?" I interlocked my fingers, propping up the back of my head as I leaned further back into the chair.

"Well on the spot, I don't exactly know."

"Do you mind me deciding? Think about it. The upside is that you'll have fun. The downside? There's no guarantee I won't throw you in a random situation. Those are some excellent odds; don't you think?"

Her eyes narrowed suspiciously at me. "I feel like I'm going to regret it but I don't have any ideas, so…"

"Say no more. There's this place I've been dying to try since I found out about it, and you're the only person I could see myself going with. It's an evening thing though so I'll have to figure out a way to fill in the blanks. Either way, you want to shoot for maybe ten, ten-thirty?"

"Doable." she nodded. My hand found its way to her left thigh, bare and firm yet soft to the touch. "In the meantime, you sure you don't want to drop by later?" She peeled my hand off her thigh and shot me a sure expression.

"That I am."

I fought back a laugh. "So is that what it is? Get me hooked only to leave me strung out on you? Interesting tactic." She rolled her eyes, clearly annoyed with me.

"It's not even that. It's just I hate feeling like it's just sex between us…"

"Naima. I can't think of a time it ever has been but I understand your take on things. Do you trust me?"

Four small words with one heavy meaning. Her face contorted into a smug expression, so a part of me already had my answer.

"Timothy. This conversation is a little heavy to be having while I have on a cape and you're staring at me with ten tons of makeup on your face."

See, that's where she was wrong. That made it the perfect time to talk about this.

"Just so you know, no is a viable response to what I just asked you. Keeping my feelings in tact wasn't the purpose of the question. It's just something I'm curious about. So I'll ask again. Do you trust me?"

"Do you trust me?" she turned around and asked. The only difference? That I actually had an answer waiting.

"I trust that I want to trust you. I'm not sure if I do yet. See how easy that was." She let out an exasperated sigh that was more confused than irritated.

"Fine, since you're being honest, here's the truth. Sometimes I feel like you're an open book. Other times, it's like cracking the Da Vinci code. I want to say I do but…we both know we met under some less than desirable circumstances."

"Right, because once a cheater, always a cheater." I blurted before I could stop myself.

"I didn't say that."

"But if it's how you feel, then let me have it. At this point in my life I have no interest in telling people what they want to hear so I'll leave you with this. Naima, I feel close to you. You're a good friend to me but it's like lately I never feel entirely sure of what I want versus what I need and *yet…* it's like I can't spend a full hour in my day without thinking about you. If you ask me now, I can honestly tell you I have no idea what that means to me. I wish there was something I could tell you that was more definitive and definite but that's just what it is."

"I can live with that. It's not like I'm not sorting out all my thoughts and feelings, I just thought it'd be nice to do something other than answering each other for booty calls."

I laughed. "More like cuddle calls. As soon as my head hits that pillow after picking you up, I'm asleep. I have no clue what *you're* talking about." I teased as she playfully kicked my leg away from hers. She removed her cape and laid it down at the back of her chair.

"I feel like I should be asking the dress code."

"No dress code. But maybe comfortable shoes. There could possibly be some walking. Other than that, your regular sexy self is fine."

"You know, if you didn't look so disgustingly grotesque right now, I would have totally kissed you."

"Don't worry. I'll be all clean and alive looking early Monday morning, hoping for that kiss." And just when I thought she'd leave it at that, she leaned in close to me, her lips only centimeters away from doing me in with her addictive kisses. A collection of low guttural snarls and hisses slipped past my lips that caused Naima to scream and jump up from her seat. That was too easy.

"My heart is beating like crazy, you idiot!" She slapped me on the shoulder a number of times before sitting back down on the chair.

"*Ow.* But you screamed though. And I don't even have the contacts in, that's just bad. Naima. We need to build your tolerance up." My phone went off with a reminder of a panel I thought Naima might be interested in. She was off in an hour and while I was enjoying this time with her, I knew she wouldn't leave without at least saying goodbye.

"Hey I think they're starting that panel on spooky creatures or something like that. I know you leave soon; you are free to check it out if you like."

"You don't mind me leaving you alone?"

"Why would I when come Monday I get to have you all to

myself? *Now go.* Before you miss the section on Wendigoes." She smiled, probably thinking I was suggesting it out of the kindness of my heart but the real motivation was another chance at watching her walk away in those sexy red boots. Sans the cape, I wasn't mad at all.

CHAPTER EIGHT

Timothy

I pried open my heavy with fatigue-ridden lids to see Naima's number and photo pop up on my cell phone's screen. How the hell was it eleven already? When I last spoke to her it was ten—nearly an hour ago and I was ashamed to admit that had she not provided me with a wake-up call, I may have just slept into next week. It was going on the fourth ring and deciding that now was the perfect time to get up, I answered on the fifth.

"Hey, I'm getting up right now. Thanks for reminding me. I'll try to be by around noon." I said in a raspy, almost unrecognizable voice. A dead giveaway that I was still laying down.

"You can do that—*Or* you can open the door for me since I'm right outside."

"Or I could do that." I replied back. We hung up with each other as I staggered to the door, devoid of any real energy, hoping she wouldn't rip into me the second I opened the door. I unbolted the locks and pulled back the door as the sight of her on the other side gave me just the jolt I needed to start the day. She was wearing this tight brown dress that was just a few shades shy of her complexion, which taking a second look, mimicked her skin tone when she was naked. If she hadn't had on a jacket to break up the monotony between the two, my tired eyes may have thought she had been.

Damn, was it me, or was this body of hers growing sexier and sexier each time I saw her. Every line, every dip and every curve on her even, shapely frame never went unnoticed and for the life of me I could *not* remember the reason of her surprise visit. *That's right.* We were supposed to be going out today. Leaving the house, breaking routine of what we were most known for doing these days. Which was screwing each other's brains out until either one of us could barely walk. Seeing her now, I couldn't stop myself from thinking…

Who the fuck needs to walk anyways?

"Tim, I'm going to kill you. It's already eleven and you don't have any damn clothes on. I know you didn't just hop out the bed." In my defense, I did have on boxers, so hope wasn't completely lost on me. I offered to hang up her denim jacket and lost the battle in my head to keep my hands to myself when my bare palm met the fleshiest part of her behind in a hard slap.

"Umph, showing up in that little dress with all that ass. Surprised you even made it over here looking that damn sexy." I wrapped my arms around her making it that much easier to fall victim to her sweet, intoxicating scent.

"You didn't have to come all the way down here; I was coming to get you. But now that you're here…" I guided her to my bedroom lifting up the end of her dress, my hands exploring her ass in her barely-there underwear.

"Now see this was a mistake. Because now I just want to bend you over and fuck you." She pretend-pushed me away despite the ever wanting desire I had to continue.

"No, Tim. We're supposed to be going out remember? You promised." Somehow I managed to pull her onto the bed and on top of me and it was there that I could feel the swell in my crotch, eager and rising to the occasion.

"All that is still happening but it's early and I'm hungry, and you're looking like the most edible thing in my house right now. Pull my hair, ride my face, tell me I can't come up until I make you cum." I said with a light slap to her ass. She took a deep breath, no doubt highly considering it but was demonstrating major control on her end when she hit me with a big, fat no.

"No," she said pressing her finger to my pouted lip. "Now put some clothes on and let's go." With zero effort, I flipped her over on her back and wasted no time exploiting one of her many weaknesses. As I kissed her through the thin layer of material that separated my lips from hers, she let out an unexpected moan, betraying the firm stance she was so adamant in upholding. I kissed her back up to her mouth knowing damn well after that, there was no way she wouldn't want to finish what I started.

"Okay, now we can stop." I threw in a sly smile. For the record, I played dirty.

"What time did you say was a good time for us to start?"

"I didn't. The fun starts when you want it to. It could be now or it could be later." With that, she pushed me slightly away and climbed off the bed. An unbuckle to the straps of those sandals came next, followed by the dress she was wearing. I bit my lip, reveling at the way her ample figure always had the power to take me from zero to one hundred in just a matter of moments.

I took her hands in mine drawing her closer to the bed. "C'mere woman." I slid down her panties, kissing her trim hips with slow deep kisses to the bottom of her navel and next pulled her on the bed. "Why are you so sexy, hmm?" I hovered over her, my lips ravenous and sinful as they glided across the swell of her breasts, all the way down to her stomach. What was it about the thought of going down on a woman that made me so fucking horny?

Was it the way her breathing became unsteady when her body

responded to what I was doing? Or was it the way her lust-filled eyes watched me as she rode the rhythm of my craving tongue? What I did know, was how empowering it made me feel. There was always a surge of power one felt, harnessing the ability to hold someone's pleasure with the flick of the tongue. Right now, there wasn't anyone more powerless than the woman bending at the will of my greedy mouth.

A tremor vibrated from the inside of Naima's thighs, to the sensation of my exploring lips. I took my time, massaging her clit out of its hiding spot, until it had no choice but to come out and play. The trick to get Naima to consider my every request began the minute I put my mouth to work, with all that it could do.

Mmm...her scent was just how she tasted. Seductively indulgent. I gave myself fifteen seconds of teasing, before alternating light kisses on each of her thighs. It was cruel, but the occasional nuzzle against her nether lips often gave me just the motivation I needed to power on forward. Nothing turned me on more than the cries of pleasure, the only thing voicing her true frustration.

"*Oh my god.* I hate when you do that." She cried, not long after a broken moan. *That's* why I did it. I knew it'd only be a matter of time before she was grinding my face up against her. Once that happened, there was little to no self-control left. Which meant I had her right where I wanted her.

Her legs gripped around the base of my neck tighter, as if she didn't think or care about whether it was necessary for me to breathe. A medley of tongue, lips and my entire mouth, kneading against her swollen clit, ever so gently. The inevitable was approaching, as pinched, wispy swears came out on Naima's end. It left me just enough time to lap the rest of her up, before she lightly withdrew.

Once I leaned up, according to my body, I was good to go. "Turn around for me." I managed in one breath, reaching for the condoms in the top drawer of my dresser.

In the time I'd managed to strap up for the main event, Naima was bent over at the corner of the bed, in jaw-dropping sight to see. She didn't even wait for me to adjust myself inside her and by the time I was right behind her, she was backing her body up against me, until I was deep inside.

Normally I liked doggy style. In fact, *like* was an understatement. While I had the disadvantage of not having a frontal visual, the view from behind more than made up for it. But Naima made it so difficult to keep the momentum long-lasting. I should've had more of the control, given the situation. But Naima had the tendency to make my dick hers, and it didn't look like right now would be any different.

One had to have the willpower of a god *not* to finish premature at the sight of a delectable ass backing up against you. A position I preferred to savor wasn't easy when Naima liked to work it her way. Still, I wasn't having it. Not with the thought of how long it was since the last time we had sex.

Granted, I knew we were on a pressing schedule. But if she were going to make me wait two weeks every time she wanted to make a point, I was at least going to make this time memorable.

Though it took quite the adjustment, I'd managed to get Naima on her side, contorted in a position that were the right parts missionary, the right parts doggy style.

With her torso turned to me, it was the best view of her face and breasts, but didn't shy on the view of her ass either. It was perfect, since she had no control whatsoever. Now was the time to play. I'd given my all to make her come before me, so now felt like the time to be selfish.

Lifting her thigh over my shoulder allowed deeper penetration, and I wanted her to feel all of it. "It's not too deep is it? This position feels good, but I just want to make sure you're not straining."

"No, you're good." She moaned, accepting each slow, breaching thrust.

"You sure?" I took her nod as her final confirmation. "Good.

I'd hate for the one position I have access to your tits and ass was the one you didn't like."

Like any other time Naima came, her body became a clenching, welcoming source of warmth that invited each stroke my hips dished out. Which was good; I didn't want her to just feel all of me. I wanted to feel all of her too. Grabbing hold of her thigh gave me just enough leverage to thrust more vigorously than the position allowed. So much blood, heat and tension met at the core of my groin, that my body had no choice but to ultimately let go.

"Fuck!" Though I'd known the overwhelming sense was coming, there was little you could do to brace yourself once it did. Once I lowered Naima's leg from my shoulder, I was in relax mode. If we hadn't made plans, I could've gone for a nap or a quickie cuddle. But at least I'd have her thinking about this the whole night. Round two was in our imminent future.

I leaned over, planting a light peck met by Naima's lips. "See? Now that didn't waste too much time, did it?" I joked, reaching for my phone to make sure the comment was accurate. Only a little over an hour. Not much to regret making time for, while it still left plenty of time for our destination.

When Naima leaned up, taking the loose sheet with her, I'd known her long enough to know the next thing she'd say. "Mind if I take a shower really quick?"

She met my delayed answer with a kiss on the cheek. "Sure. So long as I can join you."

The moment I parked I could feel Naima's eyes all over me. Confusion was a look she wore well and often and it never dawned on me how much I liked seeing her watch me with total mystery.

"What are we doing in a Whole Food's parking lot?"

"Don't like Whole Foods?" I asked in a flat tone. I unbuckled my seatbelt and in turn she did the same. "It's not that, just baffled by the shift in events. Don't mind me." That was the problem with leaving things up to me. Other than tonight I hadn't given it much thought of what we'd do to waste the time, so by now I was playing it by ear. With lunch around the corner, it only made sense to hit up the first place I could think of to do away with the hunger pains I'd ignored for the past hour and a half. Although, it had been for a good enough reason.

I took her hand and together we walked through the revolving doors into a world full of neatly, organized bins of fruit, ranging from dark red to pale yellow. Off to the side of me there was a lone cart that I grabbed realizing it'd be a lot wiser than carrying whatever we bought in our hands to the front of the store.

"I mean, if I'd known you'd be taking me on your grocery stop, I would've at least talked you into going somewhere less expensive." She walked alongside the cart as I navigated through the packaged, conveniently cut perishables.

"You ever been on a picnic before?" She shrugged. "Can't say that I have."

"Yea, me neither. This grocery trip is pretty much a supply run for the picnic I propose we have. You like papaya, right?" I said, throwing a weighty tray of diced papaya in the cart.

"I swear, Tim. You're like the most random person I know." I blew a kiss in her direction.

"Yea, but you like that, right? You see, the way I see it is, we can do what we always do and that's sit in a restaurant. Looking back and forth at menus and small talking about nothing until our food comes out, or we can get out of the restaurants chairs, conduct our own little food-a-thon, all while experiencing the great outdoors. Prospect Park's a good spot. Nice view and all that. Any objections?"

I threw in a container of pre-sliced onions, tomatoes as well as another filled with mangoes.

"Well when you put it like that, it does sound nice."

"What'll make it nicer is if you help me fill this cart up. I can't try anything new if I'm the only one picking stuff out." She rolled her eyes. "Fine. But we should split up. I have my taste and you have yours."

"Agreed. But don't get anything we can't make outside. Finger foods. Cold cuts—even sushi, if the shit is premade or you stumble across some pre-cooked rice. Oh, and if you run into some of those candles that keep the bugs away, feel free to grab some. The last thing I want to share is food with the flies." She nodded as she continued on her way to the heart of the store.

"One more thing. Try not to get lost in here. Don't make me call your name on the intercom." I joked. She sashayed past a group of people crowded around a sample stand and disappeared out of my line of vision. I entertained the seafood department, deciding on a half a pound of skinless salmon in the rare case I should find a sushi roller.

There was an Asian market a few streets down that sold them at dollar store prices so I'd be sure to stop by there, as well as one of those discount stores where I could find a basket and blanket. For a freestyle attempt, things were working out well since I always operated better on impulse. All that planning ahead in advance? Things I was never good at in my personal life. It was nice every once in a while to live in the moment, even better to spend it with a woman who enjoyed it just the same.

Approaching the meat department, I got sidetracked by a sample station, serving what looked to be a unique type of spread on crackers. I later discovered it was a strawberry-mango dip that convinced me to buy it if I was lucky enough to reach the dairy department without going overboard. I had to give it a second try at home.

"Save some, homie." Angel surprised me as he approached me

from my left, equipped in a track jacket and the tightest active pants I'd ever seen a grown man wearing. He looked like he'd come from the gym. He reached in and gave me dap.

"Coming from the gym?"

"Better. CrossFit. A motherfucker won't be able to move my legs tomorrow but I'm trying to step my fitness up. Get right before my birthday."

"That's right. You're going to Jamaica, aren't you?"

"Yup. Which, as soon as I get there, this diet's going to shit. I know once I'm there I'll probably be blazing up every night just looking for some food to eat. But then again, I might skip all that. Keep it tight for the ladies." He patted his stomach as he took another sample from the display counter.

"You know I saw Naima, too? Crazy how we're all here at the same time. *I mean* unless the two of you came together." I pushed my cart down the closest aisle only to find it was one filled with only baking goods. Nothing fit enough to bring on this venture. As I turned around, Angel was flanked to the side of me, unsatisfied with my deflective answer.

"Tim, c'mon. You and Naima— "

"Are just friends." I cut him off.

"*No.* You and Ruby are just friends. Last time I checked, Ruby wasn't putting in that kind of effort just to chill with the likes of you. Naima was looking sexy as hell, *Oh my god.*"

"I don't know what you're talking about. All my female friends are sexy as hell, so…" Although, Naima, she did wear the crown for the absolute sexiest.

"My man, it's not like I'm gonna blow your spot up. You know I don't like gossip and all that. It's more for my sanity, I just have to know. *Since last year?*"

It didn't matter what I said, he was going to believe what he wanted anyways.

"Angel— "

"You don't have to even say it in words. Just hit me with a

shrug for yes, a salute for no." As we approached the junk food aisle I stopped my cart and replied with a shrug of the shoulder. For one, I didn't have time for this nonsense, not when there was food to be bought and two, I knew he'd never accept a no, once the idea was in his head.

"*Ohhh*, I knew it," he replied with way too much excitement. "All last year I was trying to close that deal but shorty wasn't having it. Trying to say I was too young for her but your ass ain't but four years older than me."

I grabbed a bag of gourmet tortilla chips and threw them in the cart. "Sorry, man. I don't know what to tell you."

"It's alright though." he said as he swatted the air. "The two of you together, you look nice. You know, when you actually do something to that hair." Throwing up my hands in surrender, I held back a comment that would have had the power to destroy him, but what can I say? I wasn't in a roasting mood.

"For that, I'm going leave you standing here while I finish my shopping, and just so you know, shorty likes the hair, homie and I'mma keep it just the way *she* likes it. Until next time, fam." I threw up the deuces leaving him with a dismissive laugh as I stuck out my tongue.

I met back up with Naima in the frozen department as we sulked over the idea of having to forgo ice cream. To my surprise she loaded the cart up with gourmet trays of salads from the salad bar. Who ever said a picnic had to be just sandwiches?

What did the world ever do without video tutorials? With our lack of skills as sushi wrap artists, these rolls could have been potentially bad. Thanks to the help of a YouTube channel by the name of "Wanda's Wraps and Things", everything we made not only tasted good but looked good for the short while it laid in what we had deemed our "wrapping" station. It was really just the corner of the blanket we'd scored for fifteen bucks at the discount store, but who was keeping tabs?

"What about fruit kebobs? Are there any videos on that?" Naima grabbed her phone from the blanket to give it a quick search.

"You don't need a tutorial for fruit kebobs. Just take the pieces you want and put it on the damn stick. That's a waste of a video." I teased.

She brushed me off, set in her mind she was going to find what she was looking for but just as she typed it in, her phone rung. She took a deep breath.

"You don't mind me answering, right? It's just my dad." She said. I shook my head and was also a bit curious since in all the time I'd known her she talked about her father a total of four times. Every conversation about her upbringing consisted of her mother's firm hand.

She'd had a lyrical thing about her voice when she switched from English to one of her other known languages. This may have been the first time I'd ever heard this language and because it wasn't French, I took my only guess to the only other one it could've been. Her father's language, Yoruba, was it? I'd be sure to ask once she got off the phone.

"Everything okay?"

She nodded. "Yea, it's just my father will literally call me to tell me good luck with my week. I used to think it was annoying until I actually started needing some darn luck on my side."

"Let me guess, Daddy's girl?"

"No, not even. He and his wife moved down to Maryland a few years ago before I moved here. I just miss him. Nothing really going on for him and New York so they got out. Lucky them."

"Technically, so did you. Look where you are." She took a bite out of her sushi roll and with her hand shaded her eyes from the out-of-nowhere shift of the sun's rays.

"*For school*. I honestly have no idea what I'll do once I graduate. I'd consider staying if I got a better job but it's looking highly unlikely with Lisette moving too. I'd have to find another roommate, maybe even a new apartment. *Ugh*. I don't even want to think about it right now. Pass that roller, please."

Whenever Naima talked about a life beyond here, it made me that much more relieved that this thing we were doing wasn't quite on a serious level. We had fun, we didn't argue. For now, we could give each other what we both wanted. Maybe sometimes I wanted more, other times I didn't. But I knew a huge part of me would be torn once she decided she wasn't staying. At least now, I enjoyed the time while we had something a little more than friends.

"I don't think I've ever heard you talk about your dad. At least not as often as your mother." She stuffed another hefty bite of her sushi roll in her mouth as she picked the slivers of sliced cucumbers that fell from the end of it.

"That's because my father doesn't rag on me like my mother does. When I talk about her it's usually the result of her laying into me. We sort of have a complicated relationship. With my father it's easier because I didn't grow up in his house, if you know what I mean." I did. I too was raised split between two families. If anyone knew what that was like, it was me.

"What about you? I've always been curious to what your folks are like?" My forehead wrinkled, my eyes squinting as I contemplated how to describe the people who raised me. I suppose I'd had what most folks would consider a pleasant upbringing. Never had a whole ton of money but lived in a home surrounded by love and support. I was lucky.

"A little less complicated. I'm really close to my moms'. My dad, he's more of a loner type. Chill though. Listens more than he talks. I'm sure that's where I get that from. He didn't remarry like my mom did so I try to see him sometimes. Not as much as I want to since he's in Westerly and that drive isn't always something I'm down for unless I plan on spending a day or two out there. But he's my pops, I like to think we're close. Sucks to see him lonely though. He never really got over my mom, always alone. But, I suppose that's his choice." I said ending in a heavy sigh.

"Stay young he tells me. Don't know how long that will work out for. He usually gives good advice though. When I actually listen to him. You know how that goes." I lowered my back to the blanket as I rested my head in my hands, admiring the sky before giving into how heavy my lids felt in direct contact with the sun. The weight of Naima's head against my chest called for me to put my arm around her, something that by now was feeling more natural than breathing.

"This was nice, Tim. Thanks for the change in scenery."

❧

Naima

"You better not be leading me to some late night kink party." With covered eyes, Tim guided me through several turns and bends from Prospect Park. The first few minutes were cute but now I was just feeling dizzy.

"Listen. I'm about to lead you in a room of untrained tigers if you can't stop asking questions. Besides, you're all the kink I need." He said with a squeeze to my ass. "We're almost there anyways, just one more block or so. I promise."

Relief set in when we came to a stop and he took his hands away from my face. My eyes took some time adjusting to the light but once they had, I was pleasantly surprised with what I was being forced into.

"A paint bar, Tim? I'm going to need an explanation because I don't think I'm yuppie enough to fully understand what's about to happen the moment I walk in there."

"Naima, you don't have to be a yuppie to create a masterpiece. Which is exactly what we'll be doing today." Suddenly my interest peaked at the idea of attending one of those classes where a male model strips down to a sheet and you have to capture his Adonis-like physique.

"Wait, are we going to be painting someone naked?" I asked, a little too happy than I should have.

"You know; your mind is so quick to go straight to the gutter. No, we're not going to be painting anyone naked. But if you're that eager to, I'll tell you what, I can pose for you later." He said so sure of himself. I left his behind standing there as I entered this so called "paint bar" but invited his touch when his arms found themselves around my waist.

It was a quaint little studio composed of earthy brick walls with a dozen or so work stations prepared with a collection of bare canvases with tall metal bar stools at each table. We made our way to the wall of paintings on display, some of them hung up on walls; the rest resting on shelves in rows of fours. There was even a mural made up of twenty individual canvases connecting each piece making a fantastical purple and white sunset. All the paintings were beautiful but the mural for sure took the cake.

"Good Evening." An eccentric looking woman with carrot red hair and an unusual sense of style approached us. She was wearing close to ten bracelets on each wrist and for the life of me couldn't understand how she was able to sneak up on us.

Being first to arrive, she saw it fit to introduce herself. "My name's Janine," she said in a Rhode Island accent that was thicker than most natives I'd met so far.

"I'm Timothy and this here is Naima." He reached out to grab her hand to shake, and I too soon followed suit. "It's nice of you two to stop in. I've never seen you two before and I never forget faces. Is this your first time at an art class?" *Damn, were we that obvious?*

"Well follow me, loves and I'll tell you all about what we're going to be doing tonight. Let's get you in some aprons first. Don't want to mess up those clothes." She directed us to a set of coat hooks home to a few dozen aprons. We randomly choose two off the hanger and took turns tying them on each other.

With the biggest smile on her face she brought her hands together in a clap, her rows of bracelets making an echo of metal, clinking sounds that made it reminiscent of a tambourine. "Okay so with our couple classes the whole idea is to create something amazing together. Step by step I go over every last detail of how to approach the painting with little to no experience in art. If you follow my every direction, together, the two of you will paint two parts of one drawing and work to make it look like it was painted by one hand. It sounds hard but I promise, it's quite fun. Especially when we start passing the wine out. Which, by the way, the first glass is complimentary and every other after that is available at a reasonable price at the bar we have back there."

She pointed to the back of the studio and sure enough, there was a bar. I supposed *that's* why they called it a paint bar.

"Good, because I *will* be hitting that up." Tim flirted.

"Aww, he's so cute." She laughed. "If my husband looked at me the way he looks at you, boy, I wouldn't need to work nights." She joked.

"Let me know if you two have any other questions. You can start setting up anywhere you like. It's going on about a quarter after, so things should be starting up soon. You're going to have so much fun."

"You hear that? We're going to have so much fun." I mocked her as she excused herself to address the others that were beginning to gather in the class. We decided on a table by the window, the only other table with just two chairs and two canvases, whereas the other sat four. As per the instructor, we pushed our palettes together and awaited the next lesson as the class began filing up and it appeared that now we were all ready to get started.

※

"How are you two doing over here?" Janine, the instructor placed her hand on my back observing my shit portion of our collective painting. So far Tim had had three glasses of wine and his side looked gorgeous. Mine, well…It was all good when we were only painting the background but once the instructions called for layers, my poor attempts looked more like paint globs and ink blots, whereas Tim's handiwork actually looked like leaves and flowers.

"Me? I'm doing fantastic. But her," he pointed his head in my direction. "I think she may need a few more lessons." He teased. I rolled my eyes.

"I wish you would stop serving him wine. The guy thinks he's Picasso all of a sudden."

"Yea, well clearly it hasn't affected my skills as an artist." He stuck his tongue out at me. "I swear the two of you are so cute. You have to at least be friends. Lovers? Engaged, maybe?" Tim turned to her and laughed. "How about we just go with all three." He added with a wink.

"I bet the two of you would have the most adorable children." And that's when I really wished Janine would go somewhere. Some folks just loved to make things uncomfortable and because Tim chose to drink that meant I couldn't. I could've sure used a drink right now.

"Well, good luck y'all. I'll be back to check up on you all in a little while but everything's looking so far, so good." With heavy, precise strokes, Tim swept his paint brush across his part of the canvas adding the swirls required to transform the flat surface in front of him to a glistening lake. His half did look significantly better than mine. Maybe one glass of that wine couldn't hurt.

He leaned in to whisper his next words, but in hindsight, he wasn't doing a very good job at whispering. Luckily with all the conversations going on around us, in addition to the jazz induced samba airing from the satellite radio, I hoped the instructor was too engaged with other people to overhear our exchange of words.

"You ever notice whenever you're with someone of a contrasting skin tone, people are so quick to fetishize your unborn babies. I swear, I only get that with girls who are darker than me." I chuckled. "Well then that must be everyone because your ass is pale."

"I know you just love picking on me, so I'll let you have that one." He said.

"And no—I've never gotten that before." I added. Timothy wasn't the only non-black guy I'd ever dated but he was definitely the most pigmentally challenged. Dating outside one's culture wasn't the big deal it used to be, or at least not where I was from. No one blinked an eye at anyone I was ever with.

"You know; I keep forgetting I've dated more women than you." I slapped him on the shoulder.

"You're so stupid." How he was nailing all the details on our joint painting was tempting me to pull a switch-a-roo. It was one thing to outshine me but this was getting embarrassing.

"I don't know, Naima. I think with you as the mother, you and I would make some beautiful babies."

I gasped. "Yea, I'm going to start checking your condom stash. Looking for holes in efforts to try to trap a sista." He laughed, almost condescendingly.

"Babies are not the only way to trap you, woman. This tongue has been doing a great job of that on its own." Now *that* he wasn't lying about. "You better put that thing away unless you plan on using it." At that, his eyes widened, as he leaned in closer to me, all of a sudden knowing how to pass a message via whisper-mode.

"Girl, you're lucky we're in a room with all these people, otherwise I'd tear that ass up." He joked.

"Can we just paint the picture, *Timbaland.* Can we do that?" He diverted his eyes back to the painting in front of him. "But you're smiling though."

He was right. I was smiling. I probably wouldn't stop smiling until he made good on that promise.

A half an hour later we were packing up our paint supplies and comparing our two pieces of art, looking for that uniform look that might take more than one couple class to achieve.

"I think it looks nice." He said with a shrug.

"Yea, but it's like you said earlier, I need more work on my brush skills." The photo was definitely pretty. The use of pale blue, lush purples and vibrant greys to capture a Japanese inspired landscape was definitely a nice touch but I was convinced somewhere during the class I missed a step because my half was lacking some serious depth.

"Naima, stop being so picky. It looks great." We'd debated over whose house would be the photo's new owner but after some serious consideration, he'd convinced me to take his portion of the photo, while he took mine. And for good reason.

"Think about it like this. With my half, you'll always go back to this moment knowing you got to bump elbows with a true artist, whereas yours' reminds me that a beautiful creation can't *always* capture another beautiful creation." He teased. When my hand involuntarily slapped him across the shoulder, I didn't even feel bad about it. "Dumbass." I snorted.

"Why can't you tell when I'm joking, Naima? No, really. When I look at your half the first thought in my mind will be of you. If you ask me, that's better than a good morning text. All I have to do is put it in a spot in my room where it'll be the first thing I see. You know me, I'll figure it out."

In an odd sort of way, days like this—this sort of roll of the dice—was what I enjoyed most about spending my time with

Timothy. My body had wants that made it real hard to turn down nights of guaranteed pleasure, which with Tim was much harder to do. I was trying out something different with him and that meant not always making myself readily available unless it included some plans outdoors to go with it.

As much as my body had wants, my heart had needs and it needed to feel like there was more than just a casual fling sometimes. Taking it slow—or at least *slower*—was key to making me feel confident in whatever it was we were doing with each other. The thing that topped it all was the feeling I had, knowing I had all of his attention. All of his attention was proof that there was never too much of a good thing.

CHAPTER NINE

Timothy

I could count on two hands the amount of times my mother asked me for a favor. Even though I *knew* she was, but she always had to mention how capable she was, and that she wasn't an old lady *yet* (her words, not mine). But with her recent knee surgery, she was in no condition to drive—let alone walk without a crutch. It helped alleviate her stride, so she wasn't putting the same pressure on the operated leg.

Considering the son *I* was, I would've done things for her, even if she hadn't needed the extra hand or two. But I knew she couldn't handle the six-plus bags in my backseat on her own, so she'd appreciate the effort it took. I mean, it did take me almost two hours to make sure I got everything there was to get on her list.

By the time I pulled up to her apartment, it was just half past eight. I *she-hulked*(a phrase coined by my stepmom) my way to the front door in effort to only make one trip. I steadied myself to catch the breath I'd lost, lowering the heavier side of bags to the ground. I needed a free hand to reach my old key, and picked up the groceries as I disappeared into the house.

It didn't take me long to encounter my mother, limping to the living room, and crutch-less, with hair a colorless mess in some places. She earned her white streaks she'd said sometime in the past, though I had trouble trying to remember when.

"A person. Yay!" My mother cheered to herself, attempting, but failing to take a bag away from my bunch.

"Would you chillax, mom. I got it."

She shot me a look, that dismissive glance that could've only been learned from her wife Denise.

"Could you please go to the kitchen, please. So I can be the son you raised me to be."

A half smile crept into the corner of my mother's face. "Nice save, smart alec," As she wobbled in front of me, leading her way and mine to the kitchen. "You're lucky I'm so desperate for human contact, I'm ignoring the sass. I swear, it feels like I'm wasting away in this house. I'm usually all by myself waiting for someone to come home during my recovery." She said, collapsing into a pull out chair by the kitchen table.

My mother celebrated her 51st birthday a month prior, but she was still vibrant as ever. She was by no means a health freak, but she did manage her skin and eating habits well. Most people were surprised to know she was my mother, and not some young aunt of mine or something.

Appearance-wise, I'd definitely taken after her more than my father. But despite my tender wit, I hadn't inherited much else from my parents. This couldn't be more true for any two people, but my dad was a little bit country, and my mom definitely rock and roll. I wasn't either, but I couldn't help but appreciate my mother's care free take on things ever since the death of my sister. She lived for the moment up until Denise came into our lives.

In fact, if Denise didn't put her foot down, there'd be a lot more reckless behavior to account for, but mostly in a good way. My mother was as obsessed with tattoos as one got, and if Denise didn't intervene, she'd have way more than the sleeve on her right arm, and left leg.

I couldn't remember a time I'd ever had a Stepford mom. As far as I looked back, I'd always had a friend in my mother, and that was the foundation of our relationship. I know that didn't work for other people, but it worked for us.

I wouldn't want a Bree Van De Kamp as a mom anyway. Most my friends couldn't talk to their mothers about anything, but I could. The only thing I hated about being so close, was how well she read my different moods. Especially when I was in a good one.

I put back as much of the groceries as my mother'd allow, as the food she wouldn't let me put up, she'd planned to cook. She stood in the kitchen, gesturing toward the bunch of cutting knives, as I volunteered to help her prepare a stew. Shit, I was hungry.

"What are you smiling about so much, Grumpy?"

"What?" My stepmother used to refer to me as Grumpy, anytime she'd discipline me as a kid when I didn't get my way. I'm kind of embarrassed that'd I'd stomp around, like I had no home training, and mope like I thought it'd change things. But the nickname stuck, even when I didn't exhibit the behavior.

"Don't act like *what* in front of me. You haven't stopped smiling since you got here. I don't think I've ever seen you smile this much in months."

"Come on, you know it hasn't been that long. Stop exaggerating!" As I wiped my eyes of the tears caused from the releasing enzymes of the onion we'd both cut.

"You must've done something stupid." My mother started, as she brought the bottom of her shirt to her eyes. "Like, get a new car or something. Which would be funny, since there was nothing wrong with the old one you had. Or the one you had before trading the last one in—"

"Mom! Could you stop jumping to conclusions?"

"It's hard not to. You have that face. The one that reeks of *I have something new that I don't need.*"

I wet a paper towel and rubbed it against my eyes, to relieve some of the sting. It inspired my mother to do the same thing. "Just because I'm in a decent mood, doesn't mean I've done something dumb. By the way, did you want to see the new rims on my car?" I joked, before mom realized it was *meant* to be a joke.

"But really, I got this sound system that does my car justice, you should really come by and see it."

My mother cocked her head to one side and shook it, before laughing for no reason. "I hate that you got your sense of humor from me. I really could've done without that. Anyway, I'm not going to stop bothering you until you dish on why your mood is so good."

"What'd you want me to walk in angry and miserable?" I said in a laugh.

My mother sat down, unable to stand on her knee for long. It mattered not, though. We'd gotten through all the vegetables meant to get thrown in the stew, aside from the meat. I prepared the stock with just the right seasoning, before throwing everything in, as I cut the meat last.

"I can't just be happy to see one of my favorite women today?"

My mother smirked, before resting her chin into her hand. "Mmhm...you met someone."

"Mom!"

"Notice how you didn't deny it." She crossed her arms over her chest, ready for answers. "So...what's her name?"

I hesitated, but figured what's the point of lying now? "Naima."

"Are you friends? More than friends? Official?"

"More than friends," I interrupted. "But we've known each

other for over a year. There isn't a sense of urgency or anything. But she's special." I felt the need to stop myself, because I knew if I didn't correct it, my mom would jump all over that comment.

"I don't mean *'she's not like other girls special'*. More like, all the varying qualities I tend to like in people, just happen to be in one person."

Mom sat in silence while I explained how easygoing Naima was, but that she was equal parts adventurous, spontaneous and more. "Did I mention she was gorgeous? And smart too. Not to mention goofy."

"Sounds like a catch. If I had half a mind, I'd tell you to invite her to our Thanksgiving venture. You know me and ma would love to meet her." I hadn't meant to, but when my face ticked she felt compelled to reply. "Unless you think that'd scare her away or something."

"No, no," I mumbled under my breath. "But she's not from Rhode Island, so most likely, she's going back home for the holidays."

My mother rubbed her chin. "Where's home?"

"New York."

She nodded in a matter-of-factly way, as if she'd had her *ah-ha* moment. "So I suppose that's the underlying issue. I'm not going to tell you what to do. Just...promise me no matter what, you won't tie yourself down to another long distance relationship."

"Seriously, mom—"

"What? I support you regardless of *what* you do, even when I don't necessarily agree with it. Just keep in mind your last relationship. A relationship isn't supposed to drain you. It should uplift you, not bring you down. You wouldn't go over the same speed bump twice, right?"

"Mom, I'm not about to compare a girl to a speed bump."

"*Tgh.* You know damn well I wasn't comparing a girl to speed bump. Now you're just giving me 'tude because I'm telling you what you don't want to hear. Tim, I hate to see you struggle. I don't ever want to see you in that place again. If you're not going to consider my advice now, at least do so in passing."

"You know I always do. It's not like I don't have unrealistic expectations. Besides, we're not even discussing all that stuff. Right now, we're just having fun."

"Is that all though?"

"I guess." I shrugged, with little idea of what else to say.

"Okay, what are the interests like?"

I thought about it for a quick second, before answering. "Hmm...creepy as shit."

My mom balled her fist like she wanted to throw to the sky, but stopped herself. "Oh god. She already sounds perfect for you. Musical taste?"

"Hmmm...R&B and Afrobeat."

"*Afrobeat*?"

My hands made an involuntary half-and-half gesture, when something's on the top of your head, but you're not quite sure what to say about it. "It's kind of like hip hop, reggae and African music. I swear, it's dope."

"Okay. Maintenance level?"

Phew, this is where it got dangerous. "That would be high. I mean, she's not full of herself, she just likes to look good."

"Oh please. No one really minds a high maintenance woman. Ma is high maintenance. Nothing wrong with a girl who takes care of herself. I swear, before I had you and Tami, I was as high as it came. Now I'm lucky if I remember to do something to my hair. Any pics? You know I'm going to be nosy until I know."

"Not one me." I lied. Or at least it wasn't a full lie. I didn't have any pictures deemed *appropriate* on me to show her.

"Well, I guess I'll just have to use my imagination then." As once again, her face melted into Denise's look of smug self-assurance.

"If the time is ever right, I promise you'll meet her. Until then, I know that face."

Her mouth dropped, like for the life of her, couldn't understand what I was referring to. "And what face is that?"

"The one when you're trying to get into my head to manipulate the situation. Give me some time, mom. Thanksgiving is just one opportunity. There will be plenty more." I said as we both looked towards the kitchen's door to see we'd encountered another guest. My stepmom, Denise.

Remember all that stuff I said about being not like one of my parents? Well that was a lie. If anything, I'd taken the most after my stepmom. She was pure soul and had a huge impact on how I looked at the world. My best friend always joked about how she looked more like she could be related to him than me and it was true. She was of biracial, like he was. And it didn't matter that she wasn't my birth mother. It didn't change how I felt about her. She was still as much as my mother as Tracy was.

She had her thick, curly hair covered with a colorful scarf that eerily matched her light green eyes, eyes that studied me like a hawk as if I hadn't been by in weeks.

"And who do we have here? A lost stray, perhaps?" she walked further in the kitchen and rustled my hair before laying a kiss on my forehead. "Haven't seen you in over a week, stop pulling disappearing acts, Grumpy."

"Oh, it's for a good reason," my mom's eyes sparkled with glee. "He's met someone." she covered half her mouth with her hand as she 'whispered' to Denise. Denise's face lit up in a comical way that made me painfully aware that more questions were coming. I let them both know that there would be no answers until this one—pointing to myself—was well fed and packing up servings to take home. That was the least I was owed for the two of them taking the time to gang up on me. One of them alone was fine, but the two of them together? Let's just say I've never seen either one of them serve me a plate so fast.

Naima

All my things were packed and ready to go as I prepared for my trip back home for the holidays. Last year was the first time I'd missed Thanksgiving with the family in all my twenty-eight years, but come Thursday, I'd be feasting on Jollof rice, Puff-puffs, and Asun with no time to feel guilty about it. As much as I loved cuisine from all over, it still couldn't compete with my mom's goat meat pepper soup. I made sure to pack nothing but sweats in my suitcase from all the weight I planned on gaining because nothing was stopping me from hammering down on seconds. Or thirds. Hell, even fourths.

A quick call to my mother was in order since I was bringing some things that made my side of the room seem crowded and I wanted to confirm I'd have a ride home since taking the bus wasn't an option. When my mother answered the phone, she was distracted, out of breath, and barely paying any attention to what I was saying to her.

"Ma, can you hear me? I said, who's going to pick me up from the ferry?"

There was a brief pause in our conversation as my mother yelled for someone in the background.

"*Wha*? Naima, I am busy. Why have you called?" she asked in her rich accent. This was a woman who complained how I didn't call her enough, and then when I do, she's quick to get me off the phone. Typical.

"Ma, just ask someone at the house to come get me. I'll be at St. George around five or five-thirty."

"You are coming here? Even though no one will be home?" She let out a sigh of frustration as her following screams tore into someone in the background. I hadn't a clue who she was yelling at, but I was glad to be on the opposite end. My mom went into David Banner mode when she got that pissed off. Seconds later, a voice greeted me, but this time it was my twelve-year-old cousin Chiaka, who my mom had custody off. She was probably hidden away in some corner, dodging my mother's venom.

"Hi, Naima, Auntie wants to know why you called. We were getting ready to go to the airport."

"Just tell my mom I wanted a ride from the ferry. I was coming back home in a few hours."

My cousin repeated the words back to my mom, but my mother's response was drowned out as Chiaka distanced herself.

"Auntie says that she sent you a text message four days ago about how since she didn't hear from you, she made other plans. She thought it would be like last year when you didn't come."

Unbelievable. She sent me no such text. "Chiaka, tell my mom I didn't get any text from her four days ago. I already bought my bus ticket. I leave in like an hour. Why didn't she just call me?"

Chiaka let out an exasperated sigh, hating being the messenger. I had to get to the bottom of this. With seventy-three minutes before my bus arrived at the downtown station, I was willing to go anywhere they were just to get my hands on some food.

"Auntie, the message is still in draft. You forgot to hit send. No wonder Naima didn't know."

"Give me the phone," my mom finally said. I'm almost positive she snatched it out of my baby cousin's hand, too. She was in that kind of mood.

"Naima, your stepfather and I will be in Lagos. No Thanksgiving this year at home. If you want to come, you can come, but I don't have time to talk right now."

"Ma, do you hear yourself? I *do not* have money like that for an overseas trip. I barely had the cash to scrounge up for this bus ticket. Plus, I have school, you know that."

"I know. That is why I did not ask you to go." She carried on a conversation with my step-dad that made it more than obvious that what was happening in the next few minutes was more important than this five-minute phone call with her only child. Her only child who would now be alone during the holidays with no Abacha, no fried plantains, and no Banga stew to ease my pain. Why? *Just why?*

"Okay, Ma, when will you be back?"

"January fourth. Will I see you then?"

So not only would I be missing out on Thanksgiving and Christmas, but New Year's was out of the question, too. I was going to starve over the holidays. Who does this to their family?

"What choice do I have? You're already leaving. Ma, do me a favor next time. Call me, don't text!" I said through gritted teeth.

"Okay, sweetheart. Talk to you later. I have to go." She hung up without saying goodbye.

I fell back on my pillow, overtaken by a flood of regret as the past hour and three minutes were spent on packing and I knew I would never get that hour back. I shifted through my contacts, tempted to hit up Katrina to see if her folks were open to feeding this wayward child in need of some good old-fashioned Moyin-Moyin, but thought better of it. Her family was always so damn nosy and quick to report anything and everything that was going on in my life to my parents, just to have a leg up on whose daughter had the highest achievements. Maybe I wasn't impressing anyone with my field of study, but I definitely wasn't falling behind KK with her undecided-major-having behind. I wonder if I could get a refund on that damn bus ticket.

My phone screen lingered on Timothy's number, deciding whether to text or call to see what he'd be up to. My guess was that he was spending it with family, which was exactly what I should've been doing, but thinking about it, I'd never even asked him. I should call him, *I wanted to call him,* but my nerves got the best of me as my fingertips dragged across the screen to the missed calls instead.

"Everything okay?" Lisette plopped down on her bed with a bowl of cereal in hand. There was absolutely no food in this house. Everyone was saving their appetites for a day that for me wouldn't be happening.

"It's nothing. It's just…the plans I had for going back home are pretty much shot, so it looks like I'll be hanging out here. Think any places will be open?"

She chuckled. "Not any places you don't have to drive to. Why don't you just tag along with me? I hate to see you stuck here by yourself. I'm headed to Ruby's. It's supposed to be her first year organizing Thanksgiving. Don't know what that's supposed to mean, but what do you say? You know I'm not trying to be the only different one in there. It'd be nice to have someone to cling to in case Ruby's busy with cooking and family shit. You know how people are when they get around family."

My face beamed with appreciation. That could work. An invite somewhere was better than an invite nowhere. Just to be sure, I shot Ruby a quick text asking if it was okay if I crashed.

Me: *Plans fell through for Thanksgiving. Lisette invited me to yours. Is that all right? I don't want to put anybody out.* 😊

Her replies were always swift.

Ruby: *Of course it's okay. You're my girl. I want you there. I know you'll have a good time. It's nothing big but holidays over mine are lit. You heard it first.*

"She said it's okay, so looks like I'll be taking you up on that offer."

"I'm surprised you didn't make plans with *Timbaland,*" she said in an annoying singsong tone. By now, I wasn't fooling anyone with my late-night sleepovers and constant checks to my phone. When the girls confronted me about what was going on, they'd gotten the truth.

But what was the truth really? That Tim and I were dating? That we were doing…*what?* Just fooling around? The time we'd spent together the past three weeks was memorable but minimal. In our defenses, with my course schedule and his added duties at Symposium, we just weren't feeling real…*chummy.* I'd hoped to change that in the weeks leading to the start of next semester because, if I was honest with myself, it made my day when I was with him. But for now that's what the deal was. The whole situation was just making me cranky.

"Nah, I'm pretty sure he's got family stuff going on. Besides, why would I miss the chance to eat at Ruby's? She always brings in food that her dad cooks. The man does not disappoint."

"Yeah, well, you know I'm picky. I can't eat just anybody's food." She snapped her fingers in realization. "Oh, she said dress up, too. I forgot about that."

My face distorted at odd angles. *Dress up for what?* "Damn, for a place I'm going to willfully overeat at? Did she say why?"

Lisette shrugged. "Said something like, that's just how it is at her family gatherings. Told me look my sexiest."

"Yeah, but that might be just you she's talking about."

An incoming text came in, crushing any chance of that statement being true.

Ruby: *Oh yeah, and don't wear anything bummy. Dress up.*

I dropped my phone screen-side down on my stomach, that much closer to shutting the damn thing off. I finally get some sort of good news only to find out I'd have to probably wear shapewear under something I didn't even want to wear. *Who the hell dresses up for Thanksgiving?* Damn, what else could go wrong?

The phone buzzed with an incoming text.

Tim: *If I don't hear from you in the next few hours, I'll assume you've been abducted by family members and forcefully fed amazing food and held against your will to engage in good times. Either way, Happy Turkey Day. See you soon.* 🤍

I bit back a smile.

Me: *Maybe sooner than you think.*

Hours went into getting my hair in loose, cascading curls that danced down my shoulders in spellbinding perfection. It was rare when I broke out the barrel iron, but I was feeling inspired and my hair would thank me all night for all the compliments I expected to receive. As I glanced at myself in the mirror, my white, strapless eyelet dress hugged all my sinews and curves that presented me as a femme fatale, despite my usual qualms about my overly muscular arms and legs. Perhaps they were *overly*, but looking at that vixen staring back at me made me love the skin I was in. I looked damn good.

"Damn, what happened to the black dress?" Lisette snuck up behind, discarding the rollers that helped mold her coif into a hip, wispy faux-hawk onto the bathroom counter.

"I decided against it. You could wear it if you like it so much."

"Don't mind if I do," she said, as she skipped off to the bedroom. Adding the finishing touches to my skillfully applied makeup, the whole ethereal look was definitely working for me. The palette consisted of warm bronzes and flesh-toned nudes. After all, why sport a bold lip when I was going somewhere with endless amounts of food? I still didn't understand the need to get fancy, but if I was going to do so, I was going to do it right.

"Hey, I hit up the Uber. They said, like, twelve minutes. I hope you're ready," she said, hopping by as she tried to slip her naked foot into an open-toed bootie. I did a double-take in the mirror, pleased with the final outcome of my barely there makeup. Sure I was ready. The question was, were they ready for me?

Lisette and I were the first to arrive to Ruby's charming carriage house in Elmwood suburb. It was the first time I'd ever visited her at home since she lived with family, but even by the outside, it looked exactly like the house I pictured her to live in. The canvas of colors displayed a contrast of rose pinks and sharp grays, and I assumed it had to be just as chimerical on the inside as it was out.

We were greeted by two of her younger siblings, Josefina and Pablo, who shared the same tan skin and hooded but wide eyes as their sister, but for some reason to me looked unmistakably Asian. Ruby's looks were always a mystery to me since she could almost pass for a light-skinned Latina. Judging by the large collection of family photos that ranged from the seventies and beyond, there was no one way to look Filipino, especially since Ruby's family were what she referred to as *Sangleys*—Filipinos with Chinese heritage.

Just as I imagined, every room visible to my eyes presented cheerful shades of rainbow-bright walls, contemporary furniture that showcased worldly charm, and cultural antiques hung from the walls in interesting yet odd placements. I made up my mind that the rooms appeared smaller than they looked from the outside, but the massive entertainment system was to blame. That and something lined up against the living room back wall that resembled some high-tech drum machine that would have been better suited in a recording studio.

It was already five in the afternoon, and her house was almost empty. Not that I minded a small gathering of feasts, but it really made dressing up seem like a waste of time. Her sister led us to the place where all the magic was happening, the smell of searing meat seasoned with all the right spices making my mouth water with every step.

The large wooden spoon and fork set hanging from the tangerine-stained walls was what I noticed way before the people still slaving away a wide range of entrees. For a get-together so small, there were trays on top of trays of dishes I'd never laid eyes on until today, but the mother of all masterpieces was a sight of well-deserved worship. Just a few feet away sat an oversized whole pig, fried to divine measure.

I'd had lechón before, served to me shredded up and Cuban-style, but a gigantic boar staring back at you, snout and all, made you look at pork in a whole new light. I think Lisette thought Ruby was joking when she'd mentioned to her earlier that Filipinos didn't serve turkey at Thanksgiving dinner, but her looks said it all. She was horrified.

"Oh, good, you're here!" Ruby screamed over music that entertained the many in the kitchen while they worked. A bright flash assaulted my vision, and it took several blinks for the images in front of me to become clear and in-focus. Today marked the first time I'd seen Ruby in anything other than jeans, a T-shirt, and Converse sneakers. She was no tomboy, but tonight she proved there were levels to this shit.

She wore black strappy heels that made her legs look like she'd been in the gym, locked away training for months, and a gray, tailored, long-sleeved sheath dress that praised her body in the most sinful of ways. And let us not forget her makeup. On point and rocking that red lip she'd shown much reluctance to try. To wrap it all up, she slayed. A perfect ten across the table.

"It's a good thing you got here early. Everyone should be here in…" She looked at the screen of her cell phone, and her amber eyes widened. "Eh, everyone's gonna be late anyways. No one in this family shows up on time for anything."

Ruby took Lisette's hands and leaned in to kiss her on the lips. They were so damn adorable it was almost too easy to be jealous. Lisette glanced over at the twenty-odd dishes, confusion ingrained in her brows.

"Y'all sure got a lot of food. What happened to 'nothing big'?"

"Oh, I meant nothing big for Filipinos. As soon as people start showing up, it's going to get crazy. Don't say I didn't warn you."

A ring at the doorbell made Ruby excuse herself to answer it. We were both greeted by her mom, Caridad, and what we learned were her grandmother and aunts, as well as three promising arrivals. They introduced themselves as her cousins, and I couldn't help but notice that not one of them was less than model-like.

"Okay, okay. Which one of you is Lisette?" asked one with light brown skin and hazel eyes as he looked between the both of us. Lisette reluctantly raised her hand.

"That would be me."

His lips curled into a grin so devilish that I could almost predict what he was going to say next. "So you must be Naima, then. Damn. You're even finer than my cousin described you." He took my hand planting a kiss on my fingers. It was all types of corny, but I wasn't mad at all. Curveball of the night.

"Hey, get off my friend and start setting up downstairs. Jon-Jon needs help getting everything ready," Ruby said, appearing out of thin air with a slap to her cousin's hand. Who knew she was a cock blocker? "Yeah, I forgot to tell you—you might have to hose these ones down. No one taught them how to be proper house dogs."

Who needed domestication when you suffered from that much sexiness? I had to remind myself that I was only maybe, sorta, kinda single. And big emphasis on that maybe. The moment the thought struck, I couldn't help but wonder what Timothy was up to. Now that he was in my head, I wouldn't be able to stop thinking about him. After I ate, I was definitely giving him a call.

Within minutes, her house became flooded with people as if everyone decided to show up at once. "Get in the picture," someone said as she pulled me into a group photo. I barely made it to the basement without having a headache from all the flashing lights. Now I got why it was mandatory to dress up. These people were photo-happy.

Music poured from the basement as I followed Ruby's voice down the steps. It was a finished basement designed to resemble the makings of a cocktail lounge with an LED dance floor that put even a nightclub to shame. Her cute cousin was setting up his

DJ station in the far corner as my eyes lit up at all the liquor they had shelved behind the bar.

"Ruby, um…I petition we have parties at your house. Who needs the club when you can bring the club to you?"

"I told you it gets crazy. Just wait until the rest of my family starts packing in. You think upstairs is nuts? Just wait until people start eating with a little juice in them. And don't let a James Brown song come on." She looked to her cousin, plugging in a small motored buffering machine I assumed was to clean the floors. "John-Rey? I hope you have the clean versions to the songs like I asked you to. You know my mom will have a fit if everyone starts hearing the f-bomb when there are kids upstairs."

"Okay, if this is half your family, let me get my food now before I wait and get my feelings hurt. Thanks for letting me crash, babe," I said as I put my arms around her waist to shroud her in love, but she was too busy buffing the floors, getting everything ready for what was yet to unfold.

"Oh, and Naima? Heads up, don't eat anything with garlic in it. You'll thank me later."

One of the guys behind the counter served me a rum and coke, extra generous on the rum, but of course only after asking me for my number and if I was married. As long as they were respectful and polite when I told them I wasn't interested, there was no need for me to make a big deal of it. Although, her cousin John-Rey had me taking a double-take every once in a while as his eyes flirted with me from across the room, only proving I was looking as good as I felt.

As I took a sip from my drink, a set of hands covered my eyes. I prayed it was one of the girls because I did not know anyone here like that to get that close to me. I reached my arms behind me, feeling for anything that hinted at who my mystery person was, but the second he laughed and the whisper of his cologne told me everything I needed to know.

I spun around in my chair to face Timothy and was pleased with the outcome of his look. Neatly shaved, fresh haircut, and a hooded leather bomber jacket all made him good enough to eat. If I hadn't eaten already. But who said I couldn't go for seconds?

He gave me a once-over and leaned in closer for me to hear him over the music.

"Wow, you look beautiful."

"Yeah, well, Ruby insisted I dress up. Judging by the one hundredth picture I've taken in the last hour or so, I finally see why."

"Yeah, I could've warned you about that had I had known you were coming. What happened to going home for Thanksgiving?"

I told him about my mom and how I'd thought about spending Thanksgiving with my father and my paternal side, but even a few of them were going back to Nigeria for a few weeks to visit family. The truth was, had I had gone back, I would have been spending it alone probably hitting up a Chinese restaurant.

"I'm glad you didn't, though, because then I get to see you all…da-yum."

I playfully pushed him away, taking another swig of my drink. "No family dinners?"

"Nah. My family's not big on get-togethers anymore. We pretty much ride around seeing whose holiday dinners are massive enough to sneak into without being noticed. My moms are here with me. You want to meet them?"

Just then, the pit of my stomach fell to the floor. I looked nice, but more along the lines of club-worthy nice, not meet-your-mom nice. I wished I'd at least worn a jacket to cover my exposed décolletage. Note to self, you never know who you might meet. Next time plan ahead.

The upside was that he seemed eager for me to meet his mom, something I didn't rush to do with a guy I only saw as a friend.

Maybe we were headed in the right direction this time. He signaled to someone across the room, and up walked two women, one pale with dark hair pulled into a long ponytail and eyes that were unmistakably Tim's and the other light-skinned, possibly mixed race. Her eyes were a feline shade of green that were remarkably striking, and her hair a bouncy set of shoulder-length curls.

Both were about my height but looked like polar opposites. The one I guessed was his mom had a nose ring and dark-rimmed eyes with a style that was simple with a touch of rockish flare, and her companion had an uptown flavor like she was from the city. Sophisticated and stylish. She was the first one to speak, and I was surprised when it was directed at me.

"I am so glad to see another black person here. I thought I was going to be the only one. You know how it is when you get dragged to these events and you're the only one with hair people want to reach out and touch without asking first," she said in a low creamy voice. If it weren't for her crow's feet, I would mistake her for being in her thirties.

"Mom, Ma, this is Naima. Naima, this is my mother and step-mom."

My teeth clamped on my tongue hard to bite back my shock. Over and over, Tim talked about his mom in a plural sense, but I thought nothing of it, blaming it on vernacular. But in this case, moms actually meant two. I didn't have to break down why it wasn't an issue, but a quick heads-up would have been awesome.

"Oh, this is Naima?" his biological mother asked with a sly smile. The same sly smile he hit me up with daily. He took a sip of whatever was in his cup, leaving me to wonder what it was he ever mentioned about me.

"Well, Tim, gotta give it to you, all your friends are so beautiful. Oh, how it is to be young," his step-mom said with a laugh. There was fault in her commentary, though. The two may not have been in their swinging twenties, but both were plenty stunning.

"Ma, I promise. It doesn't get any prettier than this one right here."

I shot him a look of annoyance. Luckily I wasn't the only one.

"Knock it off, Tim," his mom said with a slap to his head. "I swear, he doesn't get that from me. He gets it from his father." She laughed. Even without meeting his father, I had a hard time believing that. Her smile, her laugh, even the way her eyes expressed emotion when it came to getting someone to laugh—he was the spitting image of this woman, inside and out.

"Well, sweetie, Denise and I are going to head back upstairs to go grab something to eat. It was really nice meeting you, Naima. I've heard nothing but great things about you. *Really great things.*" She kissed her son on the cheek as he returned the gesture and repeated the process with his step-mom. She shot me a wink before she took her wife's hand and navigated through the crowd. Yeah, he was definitely her son.

When they were out of earshot, I swept my hair off my shoulders. "Well, I can see um…that your swirling tendencies had to come from somewhere." I laughed, almost not able to keep a straight face.

His eyes widened at the whip of my brazen statement. "Is that your sad attempt at a joke? This liquor has you saying anything. Let me see what you have in this cup." He grabbed my hand to get a whiff of my drink. "Yeah, stay away from the dark stuff." He climbed up on the bar stool next to mine. "I like your hair by the way. It looks nice," he said, tucking the few tendrils that misbehaved behind my ear.

"Your moms are really funny by the way. I know it had to be real fun growing up."

He relaxed his posture as he shrugged half-heartedly. "Are they? I hadn't noticed." He got the attention of one of Ruby's cousins and requested a beer and lime.

"You know, it explains a lot."

"What explains a lot?"

"How you present yourself. The immense level of conscious-ness. The way you are around women. Even the fact that it wasn't news for you to mention being raised by two women. You don't put a lot of emphasis on what others would make a big deal of. Natural as breathing. I think that's kind of cool."

His eyebrows shot up. "Kind of?"

"Okay, I do."

"Yeah, well, for me it's just about seeing one of the most important women in my life happy. Denise, my step-mom, she brings out a light in my mom I thought was forever lost. There is nothing more natural than the two of those lovebirds. Except for their love of me, of course."

I elbowed him in the ribs. "Stupid."

He inched in closer and kissed my bare shoulder. It was deli-cate, but my skin tingled at the spot. "I miss you."

I folded my arms across my chest with my left brow raised, peering into him with a glassy stare. "Right, so that explains why I haven't seen much of you since the paint bar incident.."

He grimaced. "In all fairness, I try to respect your study time. You're always complaining about how stressful this semester is. And it's not even that I don't like spending time with you. I'm just tired most days. You know me, I'm useless when I'm tired.

"Yeah, okay," I finished off the rest of my drink and fought off the temptation to request another. One more rum and Coke that strong and I wouldn't be able to walk straight in these heels. Thank god I'd packed flip-flops.

"C'mon, Naima, don't be like that."

"Don't be like what? All I said was, *'Yeah, okay.'* Don't blame your guilty conscious on me." I threw in a big grin so he could see that I was kidding. He had no sense of humor tonight.

"Did you eat yet?"

I nodded and was taken aback when he got up and took my hand.

"Good, let's get out of here."

I was halfway across the room before I realized I was being led against my will upstairs. The ground floor was filled with twice as many people than earlier, half the crowd clamoring in the kitchen while the other half swarmed the living room, lined up in front of the Wii.

My first mistake was underestimating just how many people could fit in this house. They were definitely seeing my family around the holidays. I had cousins, aunts, and uncles that I still hadn't met yet, and just like here, we all loved to have a good time over an assembly of delicious food, native music, and national dances. As we stepped outside, I was relieved the warm air made it feel reminiscent of a summer night.

"You're not going to tell your mothers' goodbye?"

"They'll know I took off. Besides, it's not like we rode together. Get in." He opened the passenger-side door to his sedan, making sure I was in before he shut the door. I pulled out the black pair of flip-flops I had stashed in my purse and soon they took the place of my heels.

"Buckle up!" he said as he revved up the car.

It was a quick cruise from Providence to a place that wasn't quite Warwick, just on the cusp of the city Cranston. The roads were nearly empty, nothing you wouldn't expect from Thanksgiving Day. We rode through an area that appeared residential, peaceful and quaint, but then again a lot of the suburbs I'd visited here could be described as so. He pulled into a parking lot that seemed oddly placed and relatively small.

"Are you sure you can park here?" I looked around, hoping it wasn't some private parking, but he assured me he'd been here countless times.

"C'mon, let's take a walk. I didn't drive out here for us to sit in the car." Our seatbelts clicked off as we exited the car, and we met each other at the hood. He took off his jacket, offering it to me as he rested it on my shoulders. With the chill finally kicking in, I didn't complain. Plus, it looked better on me anyways. All his clothes looked better on me.

He interlocked his fingers with mine and led me to the public village green that was a quick walk ahead. The park was small, with just enough street lamps along the gravel walking trail to see, but the upside was that it looked out over the water, something I was beginning to think was signature for Rhode Island landmarks. It was a good thing I'd brought flip-flops, otherwise I wouldn't have been able to keep up.

I could've spent the whole time walking, but curiosity got the better of me. "So what was that thing your mom was saying?" I said, breaking the silence.

He cocked an eyebrow. "And what thing would that be?"

"Oh, you know… 'Oh, this is Naima,'" I repeated in a similar fashion to earlier. "'We've heard great things about you. *Really great things.*' Let me find out you told them I'm like the world's greatest deep throater or something. She was acting a little too giddy."

He must've thought that was so funny because he couldn't stop laughing.

"That'd actually be hilarious. I envied anyone who could actually be that open with their parents, but nah, my mother and I? Not that close. Sex talks, yeah, those were over ten years ago."

"Okay, so how do they know about me?"

"Easy. Because I've mentioned you silly. You sure you didn't have too much to drink tonight?"

I pushed him away only to have him hook his arm around my

waist to pull me in tighter. "Well, it's clear I have to pull your leg for a serious answer so you can just forget I asked."

A brief silence fell between us, but he did the honors of answering my question. "I told them that you and I are friends and that we have loads of funs together. But Tracy, she's the one you have to watch out for. That's the one who sort of looks like me and forces me to call her mom. She's got a dirty mind. I tell her we have fun, and she interprets it as having sex in every place possible. She has these elaborate fabrications when it comes to listening."

A guffaw rose from the pit of my stomach. "Like mother, like son."

"*Ha ha ha.* But seriously, I've told them that you and I are very close friends. Maybe more sometimes. I don't know, there's no rush to define or declare anything. There isn't really an expiration date on how I feel about you."

He steered me to a white octagonal gazebo, the centerpiece of the park. It was modest and open on all sides, with two matching benches on opposite openings that had a great view of the water nearby. It was all sorts of romantic.

"And how do you feel about me?"

He cocked his head to one side, standing on the outside of the pavilion, holding my hand with outstretched arms. "I care for you immensely."

"You care for me immensely, huh? What is that? Some nice way of saying we're friends with benefits?"

He couldn't hide his dismissive smirk. "No… It's a less-threatening way of saying I love you. *There.* You got it out of me, happy?" He followed that with drawing me in and kissing me on the lips, leaving my knees trembling and ready to give in to his every request. "More than what you've told anyone about me, I'm sure."

If only I could spend the night arguing with him how wrong he was about that comment. Tell him that that was bullshit. But he was right on the money. My mother was the type of person to enroll me in an all-white school and then wonder why I was dating a white guy.

Are there no Nigerians? she'd ask, which was completely contradictory seeing as how she'd divorced a Nigerian (that being my father) and ended up marrying an American. It'd never been about race with my family, and everything about culture.

Needless to say it made me want to be with anything *but* a guy of Nigerian descent, dating nearly every nationality growing up known to man. Liberian, Jamaican, Colombian, and even Iranian, and my mom was never pleased. I was at the point where my folks didn't even want to hear about someone I was dating if I wasn't announcing my engagement.

I don't want to hear about a man unless he is serious, she'd say in her Igbo dialect.

Half the time I never knew what Tim and I were. The conversation rarely came up, and as easy as it would've been to just come out and ask, I liked us when we were easy. I liked us when we didn't aid in the complications.

For months, I would've given anything to be the one he turned to or spent late nights with talking. But now, in fear of turning back the clock, I just wanted to take things one day at a time. Just like he said, there was no rush to declare or define anything. That was one thing we were together on.

"I hate how you're so quiet. What are you thinking about?"

"Nothing," I replied.

His face distorted into a grimace. "For a second there, I thought you were going to say you were thinking about me."

I crossed my arms over my chest. "So what if I was?"

His eyes widened with childlike innocence, reminding me that he was as adorable as he was handsome.

"Then I'd say you have good taste in daydreams."

It was becoming ritual for my face to pinch in the center. It was the only way to combat the charm he spewed.

"So what? No probing me on how I feel about you?"

He nursed a slow, steady gait. "Nope."

Okay, so maybe I was overly confident, but now I was a little annoyed. "And why not?"

He took a deep breath and peered into me with those deep brown eyes. "Well, because...while we're similar in most ways, we're also different in equally as many. You...you are the type of woman who gets hung up on words. That's not necessarily a bad thing because, think about it, words are beautiful. Words are entrancing. Words motivate and move people, but at the same time, they have the power to do the complete opposite. There wouldn't be millions, if not billions, of books out there if people didn't lose themselves in words. But words don't always mean what you think they mean. That's how we've been trained to perform. To say things that we don't mean. The way you kiss me, the way you touch me, the way you fuck me—" he laughed "even the way you're looking at me right now...that's what tells me how you feel about me. The words aren't as important as the feeling because words you can take back. But the feeling...it'll always be there."

We sat there on one of the benches, my head resting against his chest and his fingers through my hair. We watched the gentle waves of the glittering lake up ahead. It was just like Timothy to rip open and bare my soul for me with just a short exchange of words. Words were beautiful, but they were even more beautiful when they took on new meaning. I think I may love this man. Perhaps I always had.

CHAPTER TEN

Naima

Urgh. I wasn't feeling these closing time meetings. And on a Sunday, too. I guess since so many of the *sea-bees* failed to show up to the early morning ones, to punish the rest of us, the winter meetings were held after-hours, when the store was already closed.

Most meetings always started out with Ravinder, and today wasn't any different. He took the floor for thirty minutes, going over Symposium's goals for sales during the holidays, but never limited to that. He discussed our holiday return policy, as well as the use of gift receipts. Then he went on into a presentation on how we could increase our chances of loss prevention, as well as how to detect, prevent, and handle fraud.

December opened up a scary and desperate time for folks, and it was easy to let things slip since it was much busier than usual. All basic stuff, really. You sat through one meeting, you'd sat through them all. My semester was ending this week, so a few extra hours in my check kept my attention more. I literally zoned in and out until Martha took the floor.

She announced the major changes that were going down over the next few weeks, but none impacted folks more than reminding us Ravinder was retiring. He and Martha were good friends, so to celebrate, she was throwing a going away party that tied in with the new year. She made it clear we had to make sure we RSVP'd, so she'd know what to expect for the turnout. Apparently she was trying to secure a venue, but she wasn't sure what would be big enough for the reasonable amount of employees.

I couldn't believe that, come next year, Ravinder wouldn't be the merchandising manager anymore. I hadn't realized how much his absence would affect me until I started acknowledging he'd be gone soon. He'd always been so helpful, especially for one who had his own responsibilities to tend to. It wouldn't even feel the same without him here.

Tim was the last to speak, and he opened his announcements with jokes—the cornier, the better—to win over the crowd. He looked extra sexy today. The hunter-green sweater he wore was really working for him. Even though I worked with him all the time in the cafe, I couldn't sneak a decent look without gawking. Being in front of the crowd gave me an excuse to peek without seeming obvious.

"So you all know I'm replacing Ravinder come January, right? Since this is no secret I'm going to need everyone to do something for me." He paused for dramatic effect. "I'm going to need all y'all to stop asking me, '*Timbo, change my schedule*' or '*Tim, I need this day off*,' because come new year, I'm not entertaining any of your requests!" His statement garnered small laughter from the crowd, mostly from those of us who knew Tim was just kidding. Seriously, these *sea-bees* needed to lighten up.

"So, anyway, I'm replacing Ravinder, but I know many of you have been wondering, who's replacing me." He pointed to himself for emphasis, continuing on the tradition of the manager who took himself the least seriously. "It brings me immense pleasure to pass the torch to the person I personally feel earned this. One of my good friends, Ruby Jiang-Cruz." A few people applauded as Ruby pretended to *act* surprised. She wasn't fooling anyone, especially me. The minute Tim told me, it was like her sixth sense was a thousand times ready to blab to me at the apartment.

"But I have to warn you. It's about to get turnt up in the cafe." And his warning was for good reason. I knew the job would be hectic for Ruby, but there was no way she wouldn't find some way to make it fun.

Tim went on to give some insight on how to improve the logistics to enhance the customer experience in the store, but by then I tuned out again. I'd been there, done that, and couldn't wait for the rest of the meeting to just be over.

"Oh, yeah, so the lot of you who put your name in the letter box for Secret Santa, we're picking names tonight, so whoever gets me is going to have plenty of time to get me a gift." He rubbed his palms together as greedily as possible.

I'd put my name in the box two weeks ago but instantly regretted it. With all these new people, I was afraid I'd get someone too dense to remember to get me anything. It happened to a few people last year, and I'd genuinely felt bad for people who'd put their names in and hadn't gotten anything.

Martha and Tim went first. Then they invited everyone else to dip their hand in. When I took my sheet of paper, I crept into the corner so no one could look over my shoulder. Son of a bitch.

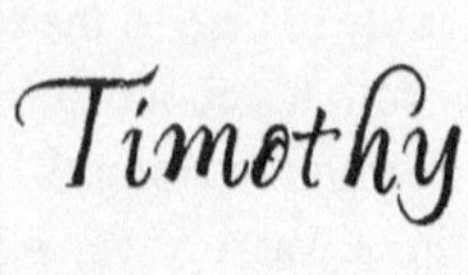

My piece of paper had his name written down in his sloppy handwriting. It almost seemed like fate pointing and laughing, making sure this would happen. I wasn't mad I got him. I just didn't know how it'd look.

Now I had to worry about what to get him. Had I gotten Bruce, I would've just gotten a gift card or another equally impersonal gift but with Timothy I actually had to put in work.

"So, everyone," Timothy said to get everyone's attention. "The deadline for leaving gifts under the tree is the nineteenth. If you aren't able to give a gift, please let someone know by the tenth. We're trying to avoid what happened last year, and all it takes is a little communication so we can switch anyone out to someone else."

I crumpled my marked paper in my pocket.

"Who'd you get?" Ruby smiled, evasive as usual.

"Like I'd tell you."

Timothy

Malls and me *did not* mix during the holidays. Overcrowded stores. People trying to sell you stuff you didn't need. Traffic. I should've gotten a gift for my moms sooner, but it never seemed like I had a free moment. I was glad when Rick asked me to go Christmas shopping with him. Could've been because I was the ride, since him and his girl shared a car. But I was just glad I wasn't the only one who'd waited until the first week of December to worry about this kind of thing.

I was on the lookout for something for Naima, too. I'd gotten her for my secret Santa, but I was ashamed to admit how I'd managed it. Between you and me, it was easy to pick the right name when you turned the flap of the piece of paper you wanted to pull out. It was my little secret, but I was paying for it now.

Between the two novelty stores the mall had to offer, there wasn't anything personal on any of the displays. The merchandiser brewing in me was judging everything, but the things that appealed to me just didn't seem like a decent enough gift.

Spencer's was full of gag gifts, but I wasn't sure I wanted to make her feel like I saw her as a joke, even if it was a gift that'd make her laugh. I considered Yankee Candle, but it seemed too whack, which would make it the perfect gift for mom number #2. She loved candles. I tried to do the math in which would be the best deal. Three for thirty-nine dollars or five for fifty-five dollars? Technically five candles at that price were a better deal, but if I could stretch it, I could get her something else, too. *Now... which flavor to get?*

She'd like a scent that put her in a festive mood, but I knew she loved oranges. Watch her get on me for considering three orange candles. I opened a lemongrass-and-orange-scented candle, and it made me hungry. Damn, a lot of these candles made your mouth water taking a sniff. An employee walked past, shooting me some evil eye look, like I was stealing every time I took a whiff. *Yeah, lady, that's what you're supposed to do.* Like I'd buy a candle that didn't smell good? I took the best-smelling candles I could find and brought them to the register. With my luck they were both on sale, so it didn't matter that I'd only gotten two.

Since me and Rick split up, he was somewhere around the mall, mostly likely at Newbury Comics, with his big-kid ass. They had cool gifts, too, but around the holidays, there were just too many yuppies in there for me. I'd go as a last resort, but I still had an entire mall to cover.

GameStop, no. Godiva Chocolate, no. Hot Topic sometimes had interesting stuff, but they'd changed over the last decade. Since when did they sell Rainbow Brite crap and One Direction T-shirts? They must've been doing whatever it took to keep their doors open. But if anything, the store catered to the fangirl, that was for sure.

The *Supernatural* section. Just what I was looking for. *Look at all this dork shit.* The folks at Symposium would probably have a field day with half this memorabilia. There were shirts, jewelry, life-sized cutouts of the characters. Damn, where was my Michonne life-sized cutout at? All jokes aside, I couldn't figure out what to get this girl. I wanted personal, but nothing *too* personal. *Supernatural* was her thing, so technically, all this stuff would have some sort of meaning to her.

But I didn't like any of it. She'd probably appreciate it either way, but a lot of it seemed so manufactured and I know I'd be pissed to get something anyone could've just got at a gas station. I took out my phone, ignoring the text message from Rick.

Rick: *Where u at?*

All this stuff had common themes, so I just typed it in my search engine and scurried through what came up.

Wow.

That shit's perfect.

Rick: *Yo. I'm hungry. Where u at?*

This guy. I decided to wait until I was home to hit up my computer. At least I had until the nineteenth to get it.

Naima

A part of me couldn't wait for the holidays to be over. It was too hectic and too messy to love all the newfound hours we got for the Christmas season. Okay, an extra twelve hours in your check a week was definitely worth it, but sometimes the stress wore you out.

My semester ended, so there was little break before the spring session. But all my free time was being put to use at work, so it was like nothing changed.

At least it smelled nice all the time. The combination of pine, cinnamon, apples, and gingerbread never failed to pick up my spirits every time I considered calling out.

We had a bunch of tree lighting events that added to the congestion in the store. Most of it was for the kids, but securing a pretty well-known midlist author for a reading brought out some teens and adults, too. I was dreading the Meet Santa event, though. Everywhere you saw those, they were always filled with kids hoping to get gifts their parents couldn't afford or asking for wishes they just couldn't give.

It was too sad to see another kid ask for their cancer to go away or for protection against a bully at school. Made the kids asking for PlayStations look so ungrateful. I'd just got out of helping out last year, but when Martha asked if I'd be an elf, I'd felt obligated to say yes. She told me I could either buy a costume and wear what I wanted or choose their gender-neutral costumes they washed and stored every year.

It was looking like I was going to be a gender-neutral elf.

Angel had everyone cracking up, though. He was rocking those tights, going extra festive for the kids. He could've left the coordinating Jordan's and fitted at home, but it just added to the smiles and laughter at getting a load of him in an elf costume worthy of a *Platinum Christmas* album cover.

Katrina approached me, unable to contain herself at the racially ambiguous Santa. "Wow, I guess Martha listened to all those complaints about the white Santa last year. Watch all the racists come out. *'But that's not tradition.' 'That confuses kids.'* Whatever."

It actually was kind of funny. I couldn't tell if this year's Santa was blasian or Latino or everything under the sun, but if kids connected to him, what did it matter?

"I see you ain't get caught out," I said, referring to Katrina in her street clothes.

"Nah. But in my defense, I did this last year. I wore my own shit. I didn't trust those stored costumes."

The costume was pretty shapeless, but I didn't think I looked that bad. Plus, the Santa hat made me look approachable. At least to kids anyway.

It seemed like it was about to be live. Between me, Angel, Emily, and Ruby, at least we'd make the best at being Santa's little helpers.

By the end of the night, I'd taken so many pictures, smiled and danced for so many kids, I thought my face would freeze into a permanent Cheshire Cat grin. I got off at nine o'clock, so I wasn't obligated to stay and help out, despite them desperately needing it. But the moment I got to the time clock to punch out, it seemed like Ruby knew as she bum-rushed me to stay longer.

"Hey! Where ya going?"

"Where do you think? *Home*," I said, trying to playfully push her to the side.

She pulled on my arm, begging me not to go further. "Don't tell me you forgot about the Secret Santa after closing?"

I *so* had. I was in a hurry, since I knew I didn't want to wait forever for a ride, especially since Tim started working later nights than his old schedule. I didn't see why whoever picked my name out of the hat couldn't just leave my gift in my locker. I'd see it eventually when my next shift started. But according to Ruby, I was being a party pooper. Guess that next bus would have to wait.

I was surprised at the Secret Santa turnout this year. Not as many people participated as much as last year, but it had still been plenty. I was always astonished that customers never pocketed the gifts. They were literally in plain sight every year, under the Christmas tree display in the middle of the store. Either they assumed we planted decoys, or Martha and Ravinder had some super force field we didn't know about that repelled customers away.

Bruce walked up, a chair in his right hand, a festive bag of caramel popcorn balls in the other as he got comfortable and secured a spot a few feet away from the tree.

"I didn't see your name picked out, Bruce," I said, curious to know what he was still doing here.

"I couldn't be bothered with Secret Santa this year. But I never miss one. The confused or upset look on someone's face when they get a crappy gift is usually gift enough. End the holiday with a laugh, right?" he joked.

Typical of Bruce.

"I hope I get something I can actually use this year. Last year, I got Bruce." Katrina gestured her head in his direction, clearly annoyed. "Needless to say, with him out of the running, at least I might see something you couldn't get at a seedy gas station."

Chatter began to fill the middle of the sales floor. The Christmas CD playing made it that much sappier, but at least people cared. From the mini-table filled with various cookies and apple cider, pumpkin spice, and regular coffee to the festive smell around here, I'd never worked at a small place that gave a rat's behind about employees.

Looked like they planned to drag this out. *Great.*

"So who did you get?" Angel said in the background, directed at Ruby.

"I actually got Martha. So you know, to keep this job, I had to get her a bomb-ass gift." Ruby said, but we knew she was joking. At least, we *hoped* she was!

Ravinder, Martha, and Tim joined each other on the floor, and Ravinder and Tim stood and silently nodded as Martha thanked everyone for participating. It was like last year, only a lot more *sea-bees* partook in the festivities. Everyone was getting more impatient by the second, but I think it was just because Justin Bieber's Christmas songs were playing in the background.

"Guess we better get down to the gift opening. Whoever got me, if it ain't a thousand-dollar check, you're fired," Martha announced as Ruby's face drained of all color. So glad I did not get Martha. Ravinder didn't normally put his name in the Secret Santa, but I'd learned by asking him that, while he didn't celebrate it normally, it wasn't uncommon in his interfaith family.

Timothy approached, a gift in his hand. I'd been able to keep that I'd gotten him a secret, even though it was hard as hell. Whenever someone'd ask me, I just shoo them away, so no one got any ideas. It happened organically. It wasn't like I knew I'd get him. Tim shook the bag his gift was in, and I winced when he looked inside.

"I wonder which someone got me."

I raised my hand, relieved I was able to give up the jig. "That would be me."

He laughed me off and shuffled through the gift paper. "Let me make sure this shit ain't a bomb, then." The bag was heavy but small and securely wrapped in blue and white tissue paper. As he unveiled the handcrafted keepsake made of solid marble, I was nervous as to how he'd react to it. It was nothing special. Its polished finish shined like a little orb, and inside its scalloped edges read the phrase:

I, myself, am strange and unusual.

I couldn't tell if he was trying to hide a smile. I hoped it meant something to him. You didn't know a person until you knew their favorite movie, and this was the movie that had jump-started his descent into all things creepy. It had to be his favorite line because he said it like it was going out of style.

Beetlejuice.

"Wow. Naima…this is…" He paused as he swiped the side of his brow before continuing on. "I hate that you're the kind of person who knows how to put a smile on my face. It didn't even have to be this deep. But I'm glad you did. I just have to find the perfect spot for it. Maybe next to the painting." He laughed.

I was curious to who got me. Last year I'd gotten a gift certificate to Starbucks. Couldn't complain—who gets to go to Starbucks on someone else's tab three days in a row? But when I walked up to the tree display, I couldn't find the one with my name on it. I could've sworn I'd seen it earlier.

"I think I got jacked?" I called out, trying to hide my disappointment.

Timothy pulled my arm, insisting he had to show me something on the walk to the time clock.

"What is it?" I asked as we stood by his locker.

"Now, I know what you're thinking." He really didn't. "You got me, so there's no possible way we could've gotten each other off mere coincidence."

So this is where it was going?

"And it isn't. I did kind of cheat, but only because I really wanted to get you something nice." He opened his locker and picked out a small square box. "I tried hard to stick to a certain theme, but it wasn't working at any place I went to, so I had to go on Etsy," he said as he handed me the gift. "I'm glad I did. Would've felt like an ass getting you something dumb while you got me something nice."

I examined the gift box with curiosity. It didn't weigh more than a few ounces, so it couldn't have been much. The box was simple and the perfect size for whatever was inside because shaking it didn't make much noise.

"Are you going to at stare it or you going to open it?" Tim said impatiently.

"Can I assess what it might be? Damn. I'm trying to make sure *your* gift ain't a bomb." I finally lifted the lid to reveal the contents. It was a box. Inside the box. A kind of…poplar wood-type jewelry box. But it did have a symbol I knew well enough to fangirl over. The anti-possession symbol on *Supernatural* that Sam and Dean had infamously tattooed themselves with.

"It's cute," I finally said.

"Well, take it out. It isn't just a jewelry box," Tim demanded.

I noticed the bronze piece sticking out. The box just fit the container it was in, as I had to tip it upside down to get the damn thing out. The bronze piece was actually a wind-up device of some sort.

"This is taking way longer than I would've taken," Tim whined, like it was the end of the world I was inspecting it.

I finally wound the piece on the side, and an eighteen-note rendition of "Carry on My Wayward Son" echoed throughout the hall, like a mini-music box. If you watched *Supernatural*, this song had you in feels every season finale.

"Wow…" I laughed, holding my palm across my mouth. "Just wow. This is…wow." Maybe it wasn't the grandest gesture, but it required the same amount of thought the gift I'd given him.

You could watch a season and consider it whack until that last episode, and then you were hooked all over again. The music box was special. No other gift would've made me feel this way. Who was I kidding? No other guy would have thought to make me feel this way.

"I am overwhelmed with gratitude," I said dramatically. I looked around to make sure we didn't have a surprise audience. "What can I ever do to repay you for this thoughtful gift?" He smiled.

"You mean other than your gift to me? *Hmm…*it is almost Christmas. I'm sure you can think of something." He added with a wink. Maybe I didn't want to be all over him at work but I already knew what that 'something' would be after he offered to swing by his place. It was a *something* I'd had on my mind all day.

CHAPTER ELEVEN

Timothy

Another long day I couldn't wait to be over with. If I kept working nights like this, I wouldn't make it to the end of the year. In just three short days, we'd be heading into the New Year and saying goodbye to Ravinder after fifteen years of dedicated service. I hadn't gone to last year's New Year's party at work, but because it was also doubling as Buzz's farewell party, I'd made a silent promise to be there this year. Plus, there may or may not have been a celebratory toast to me in wake of my promotion, and that I couldn't miss.

A knock at the door made me look up at the office's entrance. Ruby wrestled with her jacket's zipper, wearing that familiar look on her face when she was seconds away from asking for a favor.

"What's up, Sailor Moon?"

She sighed heavily as her arms hung loosely at her sides. "I know it's way past your bedtime and out of the way, but…think I could get a ride? You know after nine the buses start acting stupid."

"No need to plead your case. I would've said yes regardless.

Just give me a few minutes to finish up in here." I tossed her my car keys, which she majestically caught in one hand. "I won't be long. Just wait for me there."

"Thanks, Tim. You know I owe you one," she said as she headed in the other direction.

"Actually, you owe me like seven, but this one's a freebie," I shouted after her.

❀

It was one of those nights where the weather didn't live up to the season. There was no reason for it to be the last week of December with no sign of snow or even a jacket for that matter. I was told to enjoy it while it lasted and called a nut job, but I was ready for a real winter. As I entered my car, Ruby did me the courtesy of starting it up, saving me valuable minutes of bullshitting, and I pulled out the parking lot.

I looked over at Ruby texting away at her phone in a hurried frenzy as halfway to I-95 it dawned on me that I had no idea where I was going.

"So where am I taking you? Home or to the love nest?"

It was crazy how often Ruby's time was spent there. I honestly thought she'd moved in. I loved seeing her happy, though. We'd known each other for years, and while we hadn't become friends until she started working at Symposium, she was honest, refusing to lie to me even in the toughest situations. Women always gave damn good advice, but on the other hand, they were always inquiring. Maybe it was just my friends. Maybe it was just Ruby.

"*Haha*, very funny. I need to go home tonight. I have some family crap that can't wait. Don't use me as an excuse to go over there," she shot back. *The highway, it was.* "I know I've been wrapped up in my own shit for, gosh, it has to have been a while now. Sometimes I forget to ask what's going on with you. So what's going on?"

"Ruby, you see me every day. You *know* what's going on. My day is work, home, sleep. Rinse, lather, repeat."

"Yeah, but c'mon. You and Naima again. I know you two aren't sleeping the whole time." That we were not. "So what's the deal with you two anyways?"

"Ruby, please. Don't back me into a corner. Besides, aren't you two close? Don't you guys talk?"

"We talk, just not about you." She stuck out her tongue to taunt me. "So spill. Are y'all in a better place or what?"

"Okay, so here's the deal. Words cannot describe how much I feel for that woman. No one's perfect, but if there was a race for close enough, in my eyes, Naima is it."

"*But…*" she interrupted.

"*But* is it wrong of me to feel like I'm not necessarily in the right state of mind for a serious relationship? I like being with her and that she makes me laugh and makes me think, but the idea of being serious with someone…it scares me. Not because I don't want it but because there's a huge chance I could end up feeling like shit if things don't go according to plan. I like what we're doing right now. There's no pressure." I pulled up to her house and put the car in park.

"I think that's more or less how she feels. I really should ask her. In the meantime, don't screw up. You know I'm all for this T'aima thing." She waved her hand around as I laughed under my breath. "But I'll probably side with her no matter what. Solidarity and all. Check you later. Tell Naima I said hi," she added before stepping out of the car and heading toward her house.

Now that the thought was in my head I couldn't ignore it. I didn't see the point of going all the way home without seeing first if Naima was around to keep me company.

Me: *Sleeping?*

At 9:48, I was surprised to hear back from her in less than a minute.

Naima: *No. Watching TV. You?*

Me: *Just got off. Gave Ruby a ride. Not far. I wanna see you.*

For as long as it took for her to reply, I counted on a big fat no, but as luck would have it, I was presented with a compromise.

Naima: *Okay but no sleepovers. Whole ton of things to do tomorrow and need a full night's rest.*

I pursed my lips as I typed my response.

Me: *Why do you suck?* 

Me: *JK. In the mood for pancakes. Julian's closes at midnight. Be ready.*

We pulled up to the restaurant, getting there just an hour before their kitchen closed. The thing about Julian's was that it was the only place in this city that served breakfast items that made IHOP envious, and their vegan dishes made you question why you ever ate meat. It had the makings of a lounge with its dim lighting and if I wasn't obsessed with eating clean, I'd go here more often.

We were seated in a prompt manner at a table in the middle of the dining area and given some time to look over the menus. Technically they didn't serve breakfast past four-thirty, but since it was a slow night and the guy in the kitchen was a friend of a friend, a quick name drop and an exception was made.

Just when I thought I knew what I wanted, the picture of the French toast option made my mouth water. In the end, I decided I couldn't choose and would just order both. Indecisiveness made me a broke man.

"Well, I already know what I want," I said, closing the menu. She looked it over a few times and thankfully came to a decision before our waiter came back.

"What's wrong? Not hungry?" I asked when she ordered a mixed green salad.

She shook her head. "No. I just ate earlier, but I knew you'd call me out if I didn't get at least something."

I laughed. "You're right. I probably would've."

After a monotonous exchange of words about work, I was relieved when the waiter came out with our food. I drowned the pancakes in syrup and carved out a piece of light and fluffy excellency, which I then popped into my mouth. I needed to learn how to make these.

"So going to the New Year's party at work?" I asked to break the silence.

She shrugged. "Are you asking me?"

"Do I have to formally ask you to get you to go?" I felt strongly about the two of us not being a secret, but at work it was…well, work. A bunch of them always had their suspicions that we were involved in some sort of way, but technically since I was her supervisor, I knew I'd get accused (even more so than now) of favoritism. Perhaps it'd get easier once I moved departments, but I almost didn't believe that.

"I don't know, Tim. I don't have anything I actually want to wear. I shipped a bunch of my clothes to my aunt's a few weeks ago. Things were getting too cluttered in that room, but unfortunately it was all my good stuff."

"You mean to tell me you have nothing to wear to a party? Even if you had only three dresses, that's still two more than anyone at work has seen you in. Besides, people see you at work every day. We all know you're beautiful.

"My moms are going to be there for a little while, and I think my dad might come through. That's a huge might. Either way, I want you there."

She huffed in defeat. "Fine, I'll see if I can borrow something from Lisette."

"That's actually a good idea." I laughed.

"Oh, yeah? And why is that?"

"Because she's smaller than you so anything that's hers will look all tight and sexy on you."

❀

Naima

I hated the holidays. I must've gone to five parties since October, to the point where it was feeling like overkill. People found a reason to get together over anything, but what I really wanted to do was unwind and let some of this craziness pass me.

Who was I kidding? Passing up an opportunity to eat and drink for free was just stupid, and besides, it was New Year's Eve. My only alternative was to sit home, watching everyone else have fun. Not happening. There were too many times back home where I'd been invited out only to sulk in my bed wishing I'd said yes. I was way overdue for some fun, and Providence was proving the perfect place for it.

It sucked that I didn't get off until seven. By the time I got home, it left me so little time to do my hair and makeup, especially if I wanted a ride. I still couldn't believe this was Ravinder's going away. He was reserved at times, but I knew I'd miss his mellowness. Tim was mellow, but he wasn't that *mellow*. I had a feeling Tim was about to become everyone's worst nightmare.

Either way, I had too much on my mind to think about them right now. Ruby and her bum ass couldn't wait for me, so I'd be walking into the party alone. Excuse to be fashionably late!

I knew what I *wanted* to wear, which was a black slim-fit dress and contrasting knee-high brown boots. But in order to do so, I'd definitely need a jacket. I only wore my full-length trench coat when it was going to be windy. It wasn't really warm, but it covered all the parts that got cold, so all I'd have to do was double-up with a scarf and gloves.

I just needed to figure out what I'd do about my hair. It'd been straight all week, with the tedious effort of wrapping it every night and styling it in the morning. By now, it was a limp, boring mess. I didn't even think it was fair to call it a mess. That word implied a height and texture I couldn't control. This? It was nothing a little side part couldn't fix.

❀

Time flew when you were trying to be fly. It was going on ten o'clock. I'd planned to catch a cab since almost everyone who'd offered to drive me was already at the party. It was fine by me since I didn't want to rush on anyone else's time. I put a request on my Uber app, and within minutes, they called to confirm they were downstairs.

A random text floated across my screen.

Tim: *You still coming, right? I'll be mad if you turned down a ride just to sit @ home all night.*

His wasn't the only one either. An inbox full of ten or so messages mirrored the same context, and I wasn't about to reply to every single one. Especially since I was on my way.

When I got downtown, I took the fresh December atmosphere in. The cold didn't have the bite you'd expect from a Northeastern winter night, so my hair and eye makeup withstood the weather. I walked up and down this city every time I went to work, but I never took for granted how clean Providence's downtown was. Not to say NYC wasn't lovely, but it was easy to appreciate a beautiful setting free of debris.

The Renaissance added much more to the scene, unique in its Greek-revival architectural design. I tipped my driver as he pulled up to the hotel's entrance, and I made my way inside. The courtesy desk was quick to direct anyone who asked where the party was, but from the sound of things, I didn't need to ask. Were we at an Indian wedding? A Bollywood film set? This couldn't have been your average New Year's party going on. It sounded too hype.

I checked in with the hotel staff at the door, alongside other people who worked at Symposium I didn't know very well. It wasn't door to door, but there were a lot of people. Way more than who worked there. It was a good thing I'd RSVP'd!

"Hey, you! Everybody thought you weren't coming!" Emily came out of nowhere, anxiously bouncing on the balls of her feet. She took my wrist and pointed me in the direction of the food as she talked on and on about the spring semester coming up. It was my last semester, so I was still figuring out what to do with myself. All I knew was that talking about classes and registration and all that other mess was not my idea of striking up conversation at a party. Her mouth moved, but I was so not listening.

When we approached the catering tables, there was so much to consider and not enough time to process thoughts. Emily grabbed two plates, handing me the spare as she eyed the dishes down like she'd never eaten a full plate of food before.

"I love Indian food!" she roared.

Since it was also Ravinder's going away, there was nothing but South Asian food, and it was turning on all five of my senses smelling like an Indian restaurant during a lunch buffet. Three trays of curries—one chicken, one lamb and the last eggplant for vegetarians. There were five different desserts that I'd offend a bystander trying to pronounce. But I was really here for the naan. That delicious tandoor-baked pocket of carbs. I didn't care what anyone said—you could probably live off of naan alone. But thanks to their delicious dipping sauces, one didn't have to.

Emily filled her plate with four different choices. "Damn, girl, save some!" I teased. I packed a naan on the side of my own dish, making sure to leave a little room for basmati rice. I came across a dessert that both intrigued and scared me.

"Try one. They're good!" the lady behind me beckoned as I used the tongs to sample. I didn't recognize her, but judging by the way she was dressed, I'd say she was related to Ravinder in some way. There were a bunch of women with the most beautifully decorated saris, ranging in accents. Ravinder had family from Guyana, India and the UK so I spent a lot of time asking them about their countries. The scene was so vibrant, I was starting to think all folks who made up the Asian diaspora threw stellar parties.

"Nice to see you finally showed up." Ruby crept up behind me. She stood there, hands on her hips, studying me.

"I know you're not talking, Ms. Thang."

"I almost thought you weren't going to show until the damn ball dropped. It's going on ten-thirty."

"Will you hush?" I playfully went back and forth with her. She was just mad Lisette hadn't wanted to come. Lisette knew a few people from work, but she was too much of an introvert to be around an entire room full of people she didn't know personally again. Angel came up behind me resting his arm on my shoulder. "We were all waiting on you." he said and not more than a second after Timothy walked up to complete our tight-knit circle.

"It's not like anyone ever does anything, so the only thing to do is come to a work event." I was met with four silent nods leading me to only one question: *Were we all really that pathetic?*

"Good evening, ladies," Timothy said, wrapping an arm around the two shoulders close to him. Sandwiched between Emily and Ruby, he kissed both of them on the cheek. "Just in case I don't get my midnight kiss from y'all."

"Oh, please, Ferreiro. This is the third cheek kiss you snuck on me tonight. Starting to think you've got a secret crush on me or something," Ruby said. I don't know how the look Tim came back with managed to convey both don't-flatter-yourself and you-know-I-love-you, but that was the strangeness of them.

"Ruby, I'm only going say this once because you're my girl. But admitting attraction to you is weird. It's like saying I find my stepmom attractive. I can't express in words how weird that would be."

Ruby winked Tim's way.

"That's too bad, Tim. Because both your moms are total MILFs."

The expression that followed literally shot daggers at Ruby, as he reached over to cover his ears. "I'm not sure I'll be able to process much more without wanting to stab myself with a pen. Didn't know you were coming," he directed towards me as he picked up a small bowl and filled it with pudding. Timothy devoured me with his eyes, hoping no one else would notice but judging by the look Angel gave me, he noticed. I swear it was like ever since we'd run into him at Whole Foods there was no fooling him. He never said it out loud but it was evident he knew something was going one there. Angel was my friend, and a good one too, but whatever questions he had, I hoped he felt more comfortable pestering Tim over me.

Angel grabbed a flute of champagne from a tray a nearby server walked around with but his focus left our conversation when a girl who had caught his eye stole all of his attention.

"Damn who is shorty in the blue?" From a distance stood a curve-for-days, statuesque melanin-induced goddess wearing the sexiest peacock-blue bodycon dress and the cutest shoes in the entire room. She reminded me of that model who got famous for having a non-industry body type. *Toccara or something?* Whatever her name was, the girl Angel was talking about was drop-dead gorgeous.

"Too bad she has a baby." Emily added as we all watched a woman in a green sari hand Miss Vogue Italia what appeared to be a newborn less than six months old. Where there was a baby, there was a father and where there was a father there was little-to-no chance of the girl being single. Poor Angel. As long as I've known him he'd always been single and for him to be as cute as he was(not to mention tall)I dreamed of the day I could see him with someone nice.

"I don't know if you and Em have a table, but based on the dangerously filled plates you both are packing, feel free to sit with us." Tim told me as he gestured toward his table. Emily pushed Tim out the way, rushing to the first empty seat. She must've been saving her appetite for hours.

#thatcollegelife

Ruby's table wasn't far. Just behind Tim's or right next to, depending how you looked at it. Some of Ravinder's guests and a cousin or two of Ruby's were here, too, so her table was already jam-packed. It surprised me to see Tracy and Denise again, though. I was starting to think Tim brought them everywhere now. They greeted me with a few light hand squeezes and proceeded to provide the latest gossip on their baby boy. Ruby even jumped in a few times to scorch his reputation in high school, which struck more nerves than one.

"All right," Tim said after a while. "I'm going to excuse myself now. It's almost eleven, but feel free to keep up with the gang-up-on-Timothy happy hour."

Tim made his way to the front of the room, where he met with Martha and the guy deejaying. They both helped him adjust the sound equipment as he prepared to make a speech. I felt a roast coming on. It was Ravinder's going-away party after all. But a room full of chatter simmered down to a mild tone when Timothy tapped the microphone, sound-checked and adjusted until it was the perfect pitch to speak.

"Wow. Ravinder, I can't believe come next year, we'll be seeing so little of you." Ravinder nodded, acknowledging the comment. The woman sitting next to Ravinder touched his shoulder in a tender way as she smiled.

"Out of everyone, I'll probably miss you the most, though. Especially because I spotted you forty bucks two years ago. Now that I won't be seeing you every day, I don't anticipate you returning my calls," Timothy joked, inciting laughter from the room.

"You contributed so much of your life to Symposium that I don't think anyone is more deserving of retirement than you.

Now that you're counting on that 401k soon, I'mma need my forty dollars back, though…"

A few more people laughed as Martha took the microphone and went on into a monologue of how it was when she and Ravinder met. I would've never guessed they hadn't gotten along when they'd first started working together. It was funny how a few short years changed things. People. Relationships. Outlooks on things. It was nice to see some things didn't have to start out perfect for them to end that way.

She even spent a few minutes talking about Timothy, congratulating him on working his way up to be worthy of taking over Ravinder's position, joking about how he'd better say goodbye to sleep. I nearly cried when she added that Tim'd been the only white boy she'd known to grow up in the '00s but know all the lyrics to "Rumpshaker," a quirk that still surprised her to this day.

Between people shouting out comments and adding onto shared moments, the speech went on for nearly forty minutes. When Timothy finally returned to the table, and his mother grabbed out for his hand, admitting they couldn't stay but they'd had fun.

"Thanks so much for coming. I really appreciate it," he said, kissing both of them on the cheek. "I'm going to walk them to their car. Ruby, I know what I left on my plate. I see you." He squinted his eyes, and Ruby didn't hesitate to do the same. With a half-hour until midnight, there was no telling when the party would end. I took out my phone to send Tim a text.

Me: *Tell your moms I said goodnight*

Tim: *They say goodnight back* 😙

I should've stopped myself, but I typed before I gave my next text a second thought.

Me: *I always feel so awkward being around your moms thinking all these dirty thoughts*

Tim: *What kind of dirty thoughts?*

Me: *The kind that have me bent over and taking all of you*

Bold, I know. But if this shindig lasted all night, it'd be a long time before either of us could get away without folks seeing me get in his car.

Tim: *Trying to be a good boy, but you make it so hard* 😇

Naima: *I hope that's not the only thing I'm making hard*

Tim: *YOU. ME. HALLWAY. NOW.*

Naima: *That might be a little too bold for my taste* 😇

Tim: *Didn't mean "in" the hallway. Meant "meet" there*

"Hey, guys, I'm going to go to the bathroom. I'll be right back," I said, bowing out of the ballroom. Thankfully no one thought twice about it. No evil, curious, or wandering eye followed me out the room as far as I could tell. Everyone's attention was caught by something or someone else, nothing to raise an alarm.

Me: *On my way*

🦉

So glad I'd opted for a dress tonight. I'd almost worn a sweater and gauchos, which would have been hard as hell to get off, and to say I needed Tim tonight would've been an understatement. I didn't know how I managed to balance on a bathroom sink for twelve minutes, but luckily for us, a naughty quickie didn't take as long as our usual sessions.

I knew we wouldn't fool Ruby when we slipped in at different times, but no one else seemed to notice. Everyone else was so preoccupied by what the DJ was playing to the point where very few people were sitting down. When I got back to the room, Tim was dancing with the lady who'd been sitting next to Ravinder earlier, looking extra corny but sweet.

"Care to dance?" asked a cutie wearing a white and gold embellished sherwani suit fit for a South Asian prince. In other words, he was fine. College-student fine. Pre-med fine. If I wasn't already attached to someone, a conversation with him could've gone a completely different way. *Had I mentioned he was fine?*

Everything from pop to Bhangra played on the airwaves, and I had no idea what I was doing. Everyone was so nice about it. They didn't care how we looked, just that we enjoyed the music. I danced with just about everyone I knew. Don't tell me why Bruce always took the cake for best dancer partner. If only I'd been around for the seventies. I would've loved to see how Bruce was in his element back in the day.

We were just a few minutes from the ball dropping as Tim went around the room kissing cheeks for midnight. Earlier, everyone made jokes when we'd danced together, saying we looked too close for comfort and asking us when we were announcing our engagement. Nosy folks being nosy. We'd always been so successful at off-putting the rumors, by now it was habit to just deny it.

"Ten...nine...eight..." the room roared as we neared the final countdown. "...seven...six...five..." It got more exciting, closer and closer to the end of the year. "...four...three...two..."

A tap came at my shoulder. I didn't have time to say "one" before Tim planted his lips on top of mine, enveloping me in a full-blown kiss. It woke up senses in a way that made me feel all tingly inside. Random as ever, I didn't know what to make of it. He pulled away as we locked eyes for a moment too long.

Unreadable.

Anyone who'd teased us looked shocked. Maybe that was what Timothy was counting on? He didn't say anything for a whole five seconds, leaving me super, *hella* confused.

"Now that you've seen it, y'all can stop bothering us about it. Just friends. Just like we were last year," he joked as I tried my damnedest to fake a smile and pretend like my world wasn't moments from crashing down.

CHAPTER TWELVE

Naima

If there was ever a time I'd felt used, humiliated, or down on my blessings, it didn't compare to what I'd felt New Year's Eve. I'd spent days trying to forget it ever happened, trying to see humor in it the way everyone else seemed to do. But two days to yourself gave you nothing but time to think, and it was never a good look to consume yourself with a situation you had little to no control over. That situation in question being Timothy Ferreiro.

How I let myself get wrapped up in this cataclysm of catastrophic madness was something I kept asking myself. Every time I tried to make sense of it all, things had an ugly way of turning to shit. I wasn't sure how I planned on addressing my frustrations, but I did know if I didn't confront the issue soon, I was going to lose my mind.

"Hey, stranger." Tim snuck up behind me as I put away the books that people left up at the front registers. It was slow, even for a Tuesday, and since I'd begged Ruby not to send me home, the only other option was to go to the floor. Tim's domain.

Most of his time was spent in the office, but just because I was the luckiest woman on the planet, a dead day such as today meant more time he got to be out here trying to come up with a million and one ways to make book browsing lead to higher sales. Somehow I don't think pestering me counted.

"What's up?" I deadpanned, not that I wanted to know or cared. I wanted to be alone. He edged in closer to kiss me but was quickly met with the turn of my cheek. He laughed it off but sensed something was wrong when I didn't join him in laughter.

"Besides Sailor Moon and another guy up front, it's just us, you know? I sent that other girl—Tyra Mail, is it? I think that's the name we gave her. Anyway, I sent her on break a while ago. Come to think of it, she should be back by now," he said, gathering his brows to the center of his face as he looked off to the side.

I lowered to my knees to organize some books someone left on one of the carts nearby. He kneeled down next to me, taking a book out of my hand that I'd almost carelessly misplaced. How had I mistaken a memoir with a self-help book? Sign that it was time for me to go.

"Is everything okay, Naima?"

"That would be a no," I said without thinking. Now that I opened my big-ass mouth, he wasn't going to leave me alone about it. Dammit.

"Okay, what's it about? Is it school? Work? Maybe I shouldn't be asking you out in the open, but you don't need help dumping a body, do you? Because I don't get off until ten so that's going to be a problem," he teased.

Any other time I would've laughed along with his corny behind. But I was just done with joking, done with smiling, done with holding back my stirred-up emotions. He needed to hear how I felt. *Today.*

"It's about you, Tim."

At that, his expression morphed from cheerful to pensive as he made a *hmmm* sound in his throat. "You get off at five, right?"

he asked, which was a half-hour from now, I realized. I nodded in agreement.

"Well, if you want to talk and it can't wait, I'll take my lunch then and get something up the street or something. Just don't leave without telling me, okay? I don't want to go the rest of the day feeling like I missed something."

"Sure." I faked a smile. With no way to predict how our talk would turn out, I stood firm in needing to get some things off my chest. I couldn't stand the weight.

Timothy

I found Naima sitting on one of the benches closest to her locker. I headed toward mine to get my jacket and leave my phone so I wouldn't get distracted. It was never a good sign when someone who was usually cheerful didn't feel like talking.

"Oh, good, you waited for me. C'mon." I took her hand and pulled her forward until we were outside and a few feet away from the store. It was more apparent than ever that she was in a bad mood. I'd always thought of myself as a person who picked up on this sort of thing, but even I was baffled by her change in attitude.

"So…what did I do now?" I asked lightheartedly, hoping she would laugh it off with me. When she didn't, I thought it best to treat this as a serious exchange of words.

"Timothy, it doesn't really matter. You're the one who asked me to wait for you. Are you that simple that you can't figure it out on your own?"

I mouthed *wow* as I realized that whatever I did or said—and maybe even didn't do or say—she was furious with me and I had less than fifty-two minutes to find out why.

"Okay, so clearly I'm completely oblivious as to what's

changed from a few days ago, so please, catch me up to speed. You know I don't like it when you're mad at me."

She stopped, and after taking a deep breath, she turned to me. "Timothy, what exactly are we doing here? This thing that we're doing? You and me. What is this?"

My mind raced in an effort to come up with an answer that might satisfy her, but once a woman was in this mode, there was no better answer than an honest one.

"We're friends. *Correction*—more than friends, but friends all the same."

She nodded, but when I went to reach for her, she held out her hands, making it loud and clear I was not to come a step closer.

"You know, there is only so much a person can put up with. These past few months with you have been wicked awesome, but New Year's Eve was the first time I've ever felt disrespected by you."

My eyebrows knit together as I shuffled back. "Okay, now I definitely need a refresher course because I can't think of anything I did that would have made you feel disrespected."

She laughed. "*He wants to know how he disrespected me.* Okay for one, you made a spectacle of me in front of everyone we work with, and if that wasn't bad enough, you ended it with— hold on, let's see if I can remember this…" She cleared her throat and continued. "'*Now that you've seen it, you can all stop teasing us about it. Naima and I are just friends.*' I wanted to go off on you right then and there, but I told myself no, let me wait, calm down, take a few days to articulate the way that shit made me feel. But now that the moment is here, I can't think of one phrase that sums up my feelings better than *fuck you*. Dare I continue?"

She continued walking ahead, and wanting to slap myself across the face, I let out a barely audible, dragged-out *fuck*, before deciding to go chasing after her.

"Look, Naima. I didn't mean it in that way. I was just fooling around."

She turned around to me, walking backward as she spoke. "Yeah, at the expense of my hurt feelings. I can't explain why, but it's like you took me more seriously when your ass wasn't single. What's it going to take for us to be in a relationship, you getting married?"

My stomach knotted. That was a low blow. "That was…" I fought back the urge to say something I couldn't take back. "…very fucked up of you to say. But you have every right to feel how you feel."

"You've told me countless times that you love me—"

"Naima, I do."

"So what is it then? You love me just as long as it's on your shitty terms? It's not even what you did or said. It was the fact that we had literally fucked like two seconds earlier and then you reduced the time that we spend in one sentence. I don't care about being private. I don't want people in my business, either, but what I do care about is someone who claims that they love me being so quick to make me feel small."

"I get how you feel, Naima. I do. I hate I made you feel like that. I own up to that mistake, but not once in this four months have I told you I wanted something serious. I thought you were okay with how things were. Having fun with no drama to add to the situation."

"But we don't have to be friends with benefits to have fun." My mind welled with thoughts as I tried to prepare myself for what she'd say next. "I'd rather just be friends, Tim. As friends, I can't hurt you and you can't hurt me. I don't want to go back to the times of not speaking to one another. It's too distracting to be worried about someone who isn't worried about me. I have a semester to finish with no time to fuck around. Tell me what it is you want from me."

I knew what I wanted to say—hell, I knew what I should've

said—yet the words wouldn't come out even if I forced them. If she asked me what I wanted a day from now, I could've stated something simple.

The only thing I wanted was for the last four months to restart so I could relive the times leading up to this moment. Maybe I could make a relationship work sometime in the future, but I just wasn't ready. And now I was being put on the spot.

"Naima, right now it's not about what I want. It's about what you have it in you to do. As much as I want our thoughts to align on this and tell you what you want to hear, that wouldn't be honest. Unfortunately, I don't want anything serious right now… even if it is with you."

"Okay," she said with a stern nod. I went in to hug her, but she again held her arms out like she didn't want to be touched. "I'll get there again. It's just too soon right now." The only thing I could do at this point was to respect it.

"See you in a few days, Tim," she yelled as she walked toward central downtown.

"Where are you going?"

"Back home for a week. My mom's back in the States. Just need some time away from this place."

I couldn't help feeling like "this place" was another way of saying "away from me."

CHAPTER THIRTEEN

Naima

A few days back home was what I needed to get my mind off all things shitty with my life. When the girls discovered the details of my current trip, anxious to see NYC, they begged if they could tag along. Ruby couldn't stay the full four days because of work, but Lisette had some family in New London, Connecticut, who promised to give us a ride back into Providence if we chose to drop by. But with my spontaneous methods of planning, the only bus that wasn't booked was a six a.m. boarding, which meant getting up at four-thirty to catch it on time. Prep time in the morning with three women? Even four-thirty didn't seem early enough.

The interesting thing about being friends with a couple was that, if we weren't gossiping about who did whatever on a particular sitcom, it was rare when men were actually brought up. You never realized how many of your conversations revolved around men until they didn't. At least that I was grateful for. The next four days, I didn't want to think about what awaited me back in RI, and as premature as it was, I already looked forward to May.

Five more months of this place and I was on my way back to Clifton or just anywhere that wasn't Providence. Everyone I knew in NY could never imagine living anyplace else. I used to be one of them, a slave to the boroughs thinking that no place else moved fast enough for me. Now that I'd gotten a taste of what living away from home was like, I could really see myself living in a nearby state. Connecticut, maybe? Definitely not New Jersey. I was curious about Philly. I'd never heard anything too awful about Philly.

Four hours was more than enough time to drill my girls on how my life had run back in Clifton. I used to live alone when I worked full-time, but after I'd gone back to pursue my education, I stayed with my mother and her husband, who had more than enough room renting their double family home to qualified applicants on flexible lease terms. Right now they didn't have any renters, which meant some privacy in the apartment they'd conveniently furnished. Although, after this uncomfy bus ride, I'd be ready to sleep anywhere as long as it wasn't sitting up.

You are now entering Connecticut was the last sign I saw before my eyes shut down and sleep could no longer be ignored.

Timothy

"C'mon, Uncle Tim. Can't we play video games now? We've been studying since I got here," Brooklyn cried, closing her notebook of mathematical scribbles.

I'd volunteered to watch her for the day, and it was brought to my attention that she was having issues focusing on certain subjects in school. Like most kids transitioning from one grade to the next, she struggled with the change in curriculum, but lucky her, I was just the one to be around to get her excited about computative procedures. In school, I'd had to take College

Algebra 1 and 2, Statistics, Calculus, and Managerial Accounting, forced to see equations for six years straight. I was no math genius, but with the right attitude and tutor, I always passed with flying colors. *Did I actually miss being a student?*

"C'mon, Brook. Why don't you like Geometry, sweetie? You're brilliant. This stuff should be a breeze for you."

She crossed her arms across her chest, casting her gaze downward and pouting her lips. "Cuz this stuff is so hard. I miss last year. Multiplication and division were so easy, but all this new stuff is stupid."

"That's only because you don't know how to do it. Once you learn, you'll be finding any and every way to use reflective symmetry."

"It's still stupid."

"It's not stupid. Even so, I'm stupid and you love me. By the end of the day, I'm going to get you to love angles and lines and rays the same way you love me."

She giggled in her seat as my fingers met her sides in a tickle. I used to hate it when my mom did that, but now I saw why she did. The laughs from a tickle fight had the ability to brighten any mood.

"Now go ahead and set up the Wii so I can spank your butt in *Super Smash Brothers.*"

Her face beamed with excitement as she ran into the living room, skipping and squeeing. Little girls were so easy to please. If only women worked the same way. I wouldn't be knee-deep in troubles and hurt feelings. I knew it was time to move on and that I shouldn't let it bother me, but I was still thinking about what I could've done differently to handle what had happened with Naima.

Should I have talked more? Had I listened hard enough? Maybe she'd told me a million times that she wanted something serious, but I'd been too caught up in the thrill of being with her without the risk of putting my feelings on the line. I was coming up with all these maybes with no definite answers. Shit, maybe I should've kept my distance. It worked so well the months prior to when she'd left for the summer. Cutting her off had been one of the hardest things I'd ever done. Ending things with Sherri hadn't even cut as deep. I'd convinced myself the distance healed me when all it did was make it harder to date. I went out once or twice before I realized I wasn't feeling it. And all because I wouldn't admit that one thing to myself—that I still loved the girl from Staten Island. Why the hell did it still hurt so much?

From the kitchen, Brooklyn giggled and laughed, which was weird, since there was zero sound coming from the TV. She was up to no good. As I walked in the living room, she crouched down on the floor with my camera in her lap. It was my favorite camera—hell, it was my only camera—and I cringed a little watching her handle it. That thing cost me, like, two thousand bucks. I sat on the couch behind her and powered on the game console.

"Brook, c'mon. What happened to me whipping your butt in *Super Smash Brothers*? Don't tell me you got scared."

But she paid no attention to me. She was too wrapped up in eyeballing the camera as the sound of my own voice caught my attention. She'd found her way to the video footage.

I didn't film a ton of stuff on my phone since it was so easy to lose, but on that camera, I'd captured everything from Emily's initiation at Symposium to my graduation last June. I'd probably taped my whole twenties on that thing. The corner of my mouth quirked up when I realized who video-me was talking to.

Her laugh. I'd recognize her laugh anywhere. I rushed over to Brooklyn to politely confiscate the evidence. If there was a recording of Naima on there, I should be the first to see it. Who knew what Brooklyn might stumble across? Just to keep things on the safe side, I excused myself and watched a good portion of it in my bedroom.

So tell me, Timothy Ferreiro. If you were to watch this video a year from now, what would you want past-Timothy to take from this day? Past Naima asked me.

I remembered that day like it was yesterday. Probably my favorite day last year.

The advice I gave myself was good advice. Get over yourself. Be happy. *Was I happy?* Kind of. I wasn't unhappy. *Don't hold onto old shit*, I said. I'd failed miserably at that. No matter how much I fuckin' tried, a small part of me was resentful and mad. Mad at Naima. Mad at myself. Last spring had been a pretty dark time for me, angry for no damn reason. You always think you'll have control over situations and a lock on your feelings, but life just didn't work that way. Once I had her back in my life, I'd done nothing short of push her away. That, I despised myself for.

There was an hour or so of us talking. From the smallest of things to the most serious of topics. It was all tame and un-sextape-worthy, but it was a piece of her that I'd always have, a piece of her I hadn't allowed myself to revisit. Too stubborn, too selfish, and too stupid. I envied where we were in this video, knowing I may never get back to seeing that sort of joy in her expression. That smile—I wanted to see that smile again. Even if we never spent another minute alone together, I had to make things right.

CHAPTER FOURTEEN

Timothy

"Yes, sir. I understand that, sir." I took a deep breath and massaged my temples. The guy on the other end kept cutting me off. No matter how long I kept my pleasant composure—which, judging by my cell's timer, was a surprising ten minutes—nothing I said this guy was open to hearing.

Miriam, the store's bookkeeper (or as we affectionately called her, Flashdance, due to her love of all things eighties) was having her laughs at a nearby table as she helped me go over invoices. I made it easy as I was about three seconds away from having an all-out meltdown.

"Can I just explain something to you?"

He yelled back at me, mostly obscenities, but finally gave me the floor to have an actual conversation.

"As Ravinder, the previous manager, informed you—and I know because I was there—we're returning the ones that didn't margin profit. That's usually how it works, there's just no other way around it. The titles from your catalog were all well beyond the shelf-time we allow for titles that aren't selling. What you pay the distributor for returns has nothing to do with the store."

That only seemed to infuriate him. The number one thing I'd learned so far in this new position was that you needed an absurd amount of patience.

Eight minutes, three threats, and one death wish later, and I'd finally gotten him off the phone. A sense of relief coursed through me as Miriam patted me on the back for handling my first difficult sales representative (she assured there would be many more) with class and without offing myself. It'd only taken six months of training, twelve-hour days, and a very limited social life. Who's keeping track, right?

There were added bonuses to being head of the floor, like being salaried and not hourly. An extra couple hundred a week meant that this year would be my last year with car and student debt, but knowing me I'd just find some way to find add a new bill, like buying a new car even though the model I had was only three years old. Who could forget being in charge of all the store's sales reports? Everyone love sales reports.

The added responsibilities weren't so bad, though. In fact, controlling what came in and out of the store resurrected my love for a wide range of book choices at my fingertips, from virtually unknowns to best-selling classics. Book buying was the best part of it, and yet a part of me was feeling a wee bit homesick about no longer being a cafe staff member. The cafe was where I'd started. It was where I'd learned the most about work ethic and teamwork and all that other good shit that made it fun to show up every day.

Was I jealous that Ruby already turned it into the department everyone wanted to transfer to? Nah. When I was over there, it had been a pain in the ass getting people to come over there, let alone on a permanent basis. Most people liked to walk around to keep busy. On slow days, the cafe was the worst place to waste time and the callouts were ridiculous.

Okay, so maybe I missed working in the cafe a little, but only just a little. Or maybe it wasn't the cafe per se, but rather the chance to work around a certain someone without being creepy or stalker-ish. This time, I'd really fucked up. While she wasn't completely ignoring my texts or phone calls, all I got at this point were two-word responses and interactions at work were even lousier. She was cordial, which was more than I could say for how I would have been, but if running into each other the least number of times was her overall goal, she was doing a pristine job at that.

I rarely bumped into her by accident, and when I did, it was never alone. It made it that much harder to apologize in a private manner when you couldn't get one second of privacy. Maybe I'd never get my chance, not that I deserved it.

"Want to get out of this office and hit up the break room? You need to be around happy people, not voices over phone calls that have the one goal of killing your eardrums. Plus, I think one of the newer girls is selling some junk food from her daughter's fundraiser at school. Nearly everyone is on break it seems like. They must have the good stuff."

Miriam was right. There were so many people in the break room that it looked like a meeting was about to start. The room became suddenly still when I made my way through my usually bois-terous coworkers, which could only mean they were planning something. Right now seemed like the perfect time to make a surprise announcement I'd been sitting on for weeks. I was about to become Mr. Unpopular real fuckin' quick.

"*Ahem.* Since I have most of you in here, many of you can just relay the message to each other because I'm only going to say this once. I will not—I repeat—*not* fall victim to another Symposium surprise birthday party. Whatever money you guys spent, I hope you all kept the receipts because you will be getting your feelings hurt. Starting tomorrow, I will be taking the next six days off, which means I will not be coming to work on, before, or after my birthday. *However,* if anything you've wasted your money on is non-returnable, you are all welcome to bring them to my Super Bowl extravaganza, February first. Butter Cookie, while I'd love to see you there, there will be alcohol and I don't condone underage drinking."

"Timbaland, I'm in my first year at RIC. You think I've never seen the end of a keg?"

I grinned. "While that may be true, that's not on me. Sorry, babe." I leaned in to give her a kiss, but she shoved me away. A collection of "you're no funs" and "Breaking Symposium traditions," echoed through the room as many made their way out. Everyone except Naima. She sat in one of the corner tables, not paying me much attention as she lined her eyes with kohl liner. She probably wasn't even paying me any mind when I'd made my announcement.

I'd been thinking a lot lately about what we'd promised ourselves. Seeing me confess all those inner secrets and fears on the video—it'd only been a little over a year, but it felt like so much longer. It was hard re-watching it, especially since I think that might've been the day I'd realized I was in love with her. I could've been wrong, but it might've been about the time she'd seen me as more than a friends with benefits, too.

Either way, I hated how I'd handled these past few weeks, so up in my feelings that I hadn't seen her side of our dilemma. She wanted more, but I didn't let her know soon enough that I wasn't ready. With how scary it was, I didn't know if I'd ever be ready again, but her friendship was still important to me and I didn't want to lose her as a friend.

I pulled up a chair to her table and watched as her face went from focused (*apparently applying flesh-toned lipstick took concentra-tion*) to confused.

"I know things have been a little distant between us and I don't think I've ever fully apologized, but here I am, genuinely pleading my case. I'm sorry, Naima."

She closed her hand-held mirror and threw it in her bag. "It's cool, Timbaland. Don't even worry about it. Some things just aren't meant to be. No longer sweating it." She forced a smile, and I wanted to probe her mind about it but work was hardly the place. Plus, the last time I'd checked, I wasn't entitled to her explanations. Why was this becoming suddenly harder to do?

"I hope you can make it to my Super Bowl soiree."

"*Yeah*…I don't really like football like that."

"I know but…" I thought long and hard before I spoke my next words. "Look, I would really like to see you there. It wouldn't be the same without you. It's sorta, *kinda*, maybe like a birthday party, too, and I want all my friends to be there. Are we still friends?"

She smiled. This time it was convincing, but who could tell if she meant it or not? "I'll try, okay?"

She'd try. I suppose that was the most I could hope for.

Naima

I woke up to Ruby's playful screams and a pillow to the face. My eyes peeled open to see Ruby use that same pillow on Lisette, who was fast asleep on the opposite side of the room.

"You guys…" she whined. "I can't believe you're still fuckin' sleep. It's, like, five-thirty in the afternoon."

Damn, that was it? I was up here thinking it was after eight or something. Girl was going to H.A.M. on a Sunday. There better be a good reason for it. All at once it came to me.

"Dude, Bruce is going to be here in, like, an hour and you guys are still in the bed. What have you been doing all day?"

Lisette took one look at me and threw the blanket over her head. "Yeah, me and Naima, we might not go. We already talked about it and it's not even that serious. Well, at least for me it's not. Those are y'all's friends, not mine."

I just loved how Lisette didn't go with the plan we'd conjured up last night, so quick to bring it all back to me. All night we'd discussed how we'd stay firm. How *we* didn't want to go. And how *we* wouldn't do anything to break the pact. Nope, all that went out the window when her significant other busts in here with a confrontation.

"You can't be serious. I already told Rocketman to come get us. Both of you better hop in that shower. Let's go!" Ruby collapsed on Lisette's bed, giving her all at being obnoxiously annoying (not a stretch for her), doing everything from biting her to attempting to pull off her scarf. That sure as hell woke her up.

"C'mon, Ruby, stop playing. Go bother Naima." Lisette was on a roll when it came to fucking my shit up. Last time I pinky swore with that traitor.

Ruby's approach with me was gentler, kinder. She probably thought I'd break any minute, but I swear I wish she knew how unbothered I was by my love life dilemma. I just didn't want to go to Tim's Super Bowl party.

"Staten Island, you promised. I came all the way over here. I'm really not trying to spend all day watching the two of you sleep."

It wasn't as if I didn't want to go because I didn't feel like it. I didn't want to go because the idea of stepping foot in Timothy's house, watching him have fun and go on like he hadn't spent the past few months stringing me along in his web of confusion, was just not on my list of ways I wanted to spend my Sunday. Wasn't like he'd miss me. Most of Symposium was going to be there and I knew for sure his best friends would be, too.

Why the hell did he invite me anyways? How could I put this

whole thing behind me when everywhere I turned there was always some remnant of our time spent together. And now I had this maniac—whom I affectionately called a best friend most days—wanting me to spend the next few hours with the same wound I'd been trying to close. I was starting to think I might have to start checking references for future friendships.

Can you not throw me under the bus when we form a coalition? Will you put forth your best efforts to not put me in awkward's way? Do you have any cute friends with messy hair and crooked smiles that I could eventually friggin' fall for? Because those were all things I needed to know before I entered another sisterhood with women as clueless as these two. Loved them, though.

"Naima, I just spent ten minutes trying to get you to go with me. Don't be corny like Lisette."

"Man, whatever," Lisette spat from under her comforter.

"I'll even pick you out something to wear. All your lazy butt has to do is your hair and take a shower, which from the looks of that doobie, all it will take is some whipping and finger-combing. You know you got that good hair," she joked.

I hit her in the face with a pillow, deciding that if I didn't get up now, she would never leave me alone.

"Don't pick me out anything fancy. There's nobody there to impress." I got up and whipped Lisette with my scarf, muttering "Lo que va, viene" as I made my way to the bathroom.

At Ruby's request, Bruce let us stop by the mall to get properly suited for battle before hitting up Tim's. Bruce wouldn't dare wear a football jersey over his cream silk blouse and teal velour, military-styled blazer (which was actually kind of dope since everything kept coming back anyways), but Ruby and I spent ten minutes making sure we looked the part.

It was no secret that everyone in Tim's house would be Team

New England. Ruby proved that by trying to explain to me that walking in with a Giants jersey would be a huge no-no, but that was the burden of being New York-bred. It was blasphemous to support an outside team. Even if it'd put me on everyone's "do not talk to" list, I couldn't do that to my home. With how we'd been playing over the years, hell, New York teams needed all the support they could get.

Ruby's looks said it all, all starry-eyed and amazed by Tim's not-so-humble abode. I wasn't surprised she hadn't been to his place since he moved. Ruby spent so much time with Lisette that she'd barely had time for anything else.

Trekking our way through the courtyard, Ruby and Bruce already made plans to sneak away to the apartment's swimming pool/Jacuzzi, but the snow already started to fall so the likelihood of that happening was slim to none. Although an exception could be made for Bruce—he was just wild like that.

Even before we reached Tim's apartment door, loud bass pulsated throughout the hallway and the smell of a million things cooking made me walk a little faster. Even if I didn't want to be here, I'd definitely be filling up on food.

The door swung open with Tim's friend Marv there to greet us, looking all cute with his on-point eyebrows. If I had to give the papis anything, it was that you would never see a Latin guy with some fucked-up eyebrows. I totally had eyebrow envy. At the sight of me, his hazel eyes widened.

"Hold up." He kept repeating over and over. "Timothy, you gotta come get your girl. She's rolling up in a Giants jersey in a sea full of die-hard New Englanders, bringing bad omens to our predicted win tonight. Come get your girl."

Tim strolled up, red cup in hand and a look as shocked as his friend, the music drowning out whatever they whispered to each other. Marv retreated to the kitchen as Timothy allowed Bruce and Ruby to pass but kept me at the door.

"Really, Tim. Are you really going to make me take off my jersey before you let me in?"

He leaned against the open door, turning to check if anyone from the twenty-plus attendees was close enough to overhear. "No, I just wanted to tell you thanks for coming. For a second, I didn't think you would. I'm glad you made it." He opened the door wider and gestured for me to come in. "Besides, you've already tainted what little hope we had by wearing that shirt. The damage is done, you already fucked up."

He put his arms around my shoulders and kissed me on the cheek. It was sweet and real innocent, but it still put a smile on my face. He led me to the kitchen and told me to help myself to some food and walked back to the crowded living room.

While there were a bunch of folks I didn't know, I was no stranger to introducing myself. A bunch of the guys were either related to someone here or friends of friends, and two of the girls serving up shots were Genesis's sisters. Katrina was here, along with several others from work, so maybe this wouldn't be such a drag after all.

❦

Thirty-seven minutes into the game and Tim's satellite cable decided to black out, leaving everyone pointing their fingers at me.

"I knew you shouldn't have let her in wearing that damn jersey," Angel complained with a shake of his head in Ruby's direction.

"Don't look at me. I told her not to wear it, but New Yorkers are stubborn."

Screw the fact that the snow was starting to become something we'd regret going out in a little later and that the weather had a huge impact on most satellite dish performances. It was just easier to blame the girl in the Giants jersey. Bruce and Rick excused themselves from the room, Bruce blaming leaving something in his car.

"Isn't there anything you can do to fix it?" someone cried, but the downside to satellite cable was that you couldn't predict when it'd come back on when the weather was wonky. KC ran to the window and confirmed it to be true, but folks were still giving me the side-eye for repping my stomping grounds.

A few of us checked our phones to get the latest updates, but Tim's Internet provider was linked to the damn cable so we weren't able to tap into high-speed connections. Tim stood and turned on his PS4.

"I don't know about y'all, but I'm about to play *Madden 16* or something. I'm pissed I can't see the commercials, but I can't spend the night not seeing anything football-y."

All the lights in the room clicked off with an exception for the TV, which made Timothy jump up, worried that the power went out, too. He slapped his forehead as Rick and Bruce each held a side of an enormous cake, lit with twenty-seven individual candles as we all joined in to sing "Happy Birthday." This time I'd been in on the planning. I'd even got him something. Nothing crazy and clearly not as special as the thought I'd put into his Christmas gift, but at least I wouldn't be singled out like last year.

We all gathered by the coffee table as the boys laid the cake down. Tim certainly wasn't upset like last year. In fact, he was all smiles and giggles at the sight.

"Aw, you really shouldn't have. Just kidding. You really should have. But did you really have to put all twenty-seven candles, though?"

"Oh, stop whining and make your damn wish," Bruce replied. The whole ride here he confessed how he was going to demolish that cake. Guess he was trying to get a move on things.

Tim's eyes rolled off to the side as he took his sweet time contemplating what to wish for. Then he looked at me and held my eyes. It was sort of exclusive, almost like we were both in on an inside joke, but everyone was so into everything else, no one even noticed. Annoyingly slow, he blew out all the candles.

"Okay, now it's dark in here. Someone turn on the light or something."

The lights flicked back on as piece by piece the cake disappeared until it was just a quarter of its old self.

"Time for *Madden*," Tim said, tinkering with the game controller.

"*Noooo*. Play something we can all do. It's gonna be boring watching you all play those stupid games. Don't you have any dance games? Or karaoke games?" Katrina cried.

Tim's eyebrows cocked up. "Now that seems like a good idea. I could use some birthday laughs. Unfortunately, the games I have, there aren't any songs people would actually want to sing. It's all Taylor Swift and Katy Perry or, like, slow stuff. I only play them when Rick's daughter stops by. She loves them."

"You do know you can make your own karaoke games, right? I have this software on my laptop. I bought it like a minute ago because someone at my job talked me into it. Basically you sync it to your PC's library and the technology it uses detects the lyrics from the music's database." Marv suggested.

"Um…why do you have that conveniently on you?" Tim asked like he didn't know his friend was capable of such oddity.

"I carry my piece everywhere because I need it for work. Plus, after I lost my phone, I've been paranoid about losing other shit."

"Yeah, okay. Set it up then. Is that cool with everyone else? Seems like the snow is coming down out there, and since I have no idea if the cable's coming back, we might as well have a little fun. Something that doesn't require Wi-Fi. Who's down? Say aye."

With no other choice, fourteen out of twenty-one hands went up, including mine.

Marv was a whiz at the high-tech stuff. In minutes, he'd hooked up his Mac to Tim's TV, and with a database full of modern songs, everyone was practically fighting each other on who wanted to look like a fool first. I had the singing voice of a frog so there was no way I'd volunteer to make a spectacle of myself, but I almost lost my shit when Ruby, Genesis, and Katrina laid down a Wilson Phillips song. I wasn't sure what was more suspect—their performance or the fact that Marv had a Wilson Phillips song on his playlist. Dude was mostly into music in Spanish.

With a fierceness that couldn't be matched, Rocketman belted the hell out of "Another One Bites the Dust" by Queen. Every time he hit a high note, it sent the entire room into a frenzy. Was I wrong for thinking that was the perfect song for him? Either way, I loved that song, and I loved him invoking the spirit of Freddie Mercury to sing it.

"You guys, this is highly entertaining, but I have not seen any dedications, no serenades. All of y'all are just singing to empty spaces. Except you, Bruce, you brought the house down." Tim said.

Bruce bowed at the compliment like he was the King of Rock himself.

"I wanna feel like I'm at a Janet Jackson concert, where she brings someone onstage and makes them feel it. Genesis, we can start with you. I already know you can put on a show. Only for me, though, only for me," he joked as his friends smothered him in couch pillows.

No reason to be jealous. He was only playing and it wasn't like that with us anymore. Besides, he always joked around like that with all the girls, especially Genesis.

Rick was probably one of the worst singers I'd ever had the pleasure of listening to. After pulling one of Genesis's sisters up from her seat to dedicate his rendition of Stevie Wonder's "Always," I wondered if I'd ever listen to Stevie Wonder again. Her sister looked as though she wanted to laugh in his face but tried her best to be polite. That didn't stop the rest of us from booing and laughing. So far Bruce was still the stand out for the night, but who knows? Maybe he got lucky with his song choice.

"Who needs Super Bowl commercials? You have no idea how entertainingly horrible you all are." Tim laughed.

When I refused to sing for the third time, the only other person who hadn't embarrassed themselves was Timothy. Unlike me, he was open and amped for the challenge. He was silly like that. He'd probably butcher the song, just to get a laugh.

"I got just the song for you," Marv announced, maneuvering the controller until he settled on one. The first few seconds played, and nearly every person there burst out in laughter at the wailing intro anyone born after '87 knew too well. "Knockin' the Boots" by H-Town. I hoped I wasn't alone on this one, but I loved that song.

Timothy stood up in a fitty protest. "Oh, no, I'm not drunk enough for that song."

"Nope, you gotta do it. We all did." Rick said.

"Yeah, to entertain me. On *my* birthday."

Angel offered to sing the song with him, and surprisingly his friend Bobby volunteered for the last part of the song.

"All right, all right. But Du-Wop, you got first," Timothy said, handing him the lone mic. Marv restarted the track, and Angel had no issue with belting out that first verse. Matter of fact, he probably overdid it, but there was no denying the boy could sing.

We all laughed when he chose Rocketman to sing his portion to. Faithful to his beloved decade, he probably didn't know a song after 1979.

"I was so sure you'd dedicate your part to me. I'm hurt," Katrina said with pouted lips.

"Aww, I got you next time," he said as he leaned in and kissed Katrina on the cheek.

The track still played and Timothy was up. He looked nervous, like he didn't even want to be here, but the way his friends kept on him to sing, he had no choice. For his sake, I hoped he wasn't terrible.

"And sing that shit right or we starting the track over," Rick shouted over the music. Yeah, by now Tim was looking so annoyed.

The sound that resonated from Timothy's vocal chords was something I wasn't even aware could leave Timothy's mouth. A blend of measured cadence with pain-invoked soul and even a little blues mixed in. Some called it blue-eyed soul—I just called it talent.

"You better pick someone to sing to. I know you wasn't talkin' all that mess to be singing to the goddamn air," KC shouted.

Tim looked between Genesis and Ruby but surprised me when he took my hand instead, kneeling down in front of me. He sang the first line of the second verse, looking deep into my eyes with an intensity that made me look away for a second. As cheesy as it was, I did feel like one of those women during concerts who got pulled from the audience to get privately sung to on the stage. Something about this song, something about the way he lingered on the lyrics, and something about the way he looked at me brought me back to why I'd fallen for him in the first place.

Every time he looked at me, I saw something behind those two dark eyes. I felt something real, something honest, and something beyond my comprehension. Before today, I didn't know he could still look at me like that. I didn't want him to stop looking at me like that. I didn't want him to stop.

CHAPTER FIFTEEN

Timothy

Everyone had begun to start clearing out at eleven o'clock. The snow was getting really bad out so I couldn't blame them, but the way they left my house, I wasn't about to let them leave without saying shit.

"Um excuse me, so not one of y'all are going to stick around to help straighten this shit up? Like really, none?" I unfolded a trash bag and picked up a few beer bottles closest to my feet. Rick steadied me by the shoulders, knowing I was this close to going off.

"Tim, it's about to be hard as hell to drive out there. Ain't nobody here about to be snowed in for you." Rick said.

"Plus people got work in the morning," Genesis added, yet no one had asked her. They all helped fuck shit up, though. This was some fucking bullshit.

In the corner of the room, Bruce stashed a quarter-filled bottle of cognac in his pocket in an attempt to be on some stealth status. Before he got past me, I held out my hand, and he forked up the goods.

Naima took off her jacket and laid it across her arm. "Hey, I'm riding with Rocketman and Sailor Moon, but if you take me home, I'll help you clean up."

I pointed to her and blurted the first thing to come to my mind. "Done." Maybe I'd regret it later, but I really didn't want to be stuck here cleaning by myself. "See? A few of you can learn a thing or two from Naima when it comes to teamwork. I'm going to remember this for those of you that work with me. The rest of you guys got off easy today."

Genesis walked up to me and reached in for a hug and a kiss on the cheek. "Whatever. You know Staten Island ain't got nothing else better to do."

Naima stuck up her middle finger as Genesis proceeded to tackle her with a hug. That was how we handled our battles at work—with hugs and hangovers.

Ruby was the last one out as always, coming from the hallway, pulling up her pants to her lower waist. "Woo… All that liquor got a girl running to the bathroom. Glad my ass isn't driving."

She leaned into hug me, but I took a step back. "Girl, I hope you washed your hands first. Nah, I'm just playing. Gimme my kiss."

She hit me across the chest but gave in and pressed her lips to my cheek. "Stupid. Hey, Staten Island, you coming?"

"It's cool. I told Tim I'd help him straighten up. He's giving me a ride home."

A smile crept up the side of Ruby's mouth as she looked between both of us. "You two be good, okay?"

I winked. Wasn't I always?

After seeing Ruby out, I turned to Naima. She'd gathered her hair in a high ponytail, ready to work. I kicked around at the junk that somehow materialized under my feet, gearing myself up to take the room with the biggest mess just to give her somewhere easy to start with.

"So do you want to hit up the kitchen? It's not so bad in there. If you finish up before me, you can come and help me in here."

She held up both of her thumbs and pranced into the kitchen. The next few minutes, only the sound of cans and bottles filling up my trash bag kept me company. When Naima started carrying on a conversation, I was relieved to find out she hadn't gotten nabbed by a sink troll or something. Plus, it was nice hearing someone's voice after minutes of silence.

"Hey, Tim?"

"Yeah?"

"You know, I didn't know you could sing."

"When will you realize I'm full of surprises?"

It wasn't something I shared with the world. I didn't remember that far back, but my mom said, when my sister was healthy, she sang all the time. Around the house. Waiting in line at the grocery store. Even when my mom took turns beating us when we were naughty. She'd always found a reason to sing. I think it made my mother sad when she'd learned I had a voice on me, too. Singing opened old wounds for my mom and I hated seeing her sad. So I didn't advertise it.

"Did you visit her grave this year?"

I nodded but then realized Naima couldn't see me. "Yup. I posted pics on IG, like I do all the time. I mean, if you're still following me anyways." She hadn't liked or commented on a picture in months. Maybe she hadn't signed on in months.

"Hey, do you know your Wi-Fi is back on?"

I skated to the couch and pulled my laptop from underneath it. It booted on, and just like she said, the Internet was working. I turned on the TV in the living room, but because of the stupid satellite, I was still without cable for the night. At least I had Internet, which meant I had Hulu and Netflix. Must fight the urge to suggest shows to Naima. Must fight the urge.

"Okay, so I know we're supposed to be working but...now

that I have you alone, I wanted to tell you I have just the show for you."

Naima was the only person I knew who got into horror and all that gory stuff I liked, even the cheesy slasher crap. People straight up refused to watch them with me, and I was a social binge watcher. It was way more entertaining watching something nuts with another person. Especially her, her reactions. Man, I loved her reactions.

"And what show might that be? Because you stay introducing me to some crazy shit."

"If you want to take a quick break, I'd rather show you." I made myself comfortable at one end of the couch. Moments later, Naima sat down on the other end. It was strange having her in my house after our last little disagreement and more mind-boggling that she even chose to be alone with me. I knew that I fucked up big-time in the past, so it was cool that we could have these moments again. Just me, her, and flesh-eating zombies.

She took one look at the loading screen and cringed. "Now you did not say it was *The Walking Dead*."

I made this promise to myself that no matter how many people hyped this show, I would not give in and watch it until they released *at least* the fifth season. It took a lot of patience and willpower, but with it being on its sixth season, I could drown in its greatness for eighty-three episodes of marathon madness.

"Before you say no, consider this. We both know how you love *Supernatural*, right? Well, I have to tell you this one's way better and you want to know why? Katana-wielding Michonne. Plus, I hear if you stick around, there's tons of character development, characters of color who are ten times better than Rick Grimes, and two—not just one, but *two*—black women who are both ill as fuck. Oh, and a whole lot of killing. Doesn't that sound better than *Supernatural*?"

She rolled her eyes and nodded. "Maybe. Have you watched it?"

"Nope."

She melted into the couch and kicked off her boots. I'd been waiting for the right occasion to bust out this gem and couldn't think of a better time than now.

"As long as you haven't seen it, I'm in. Fair warning, though. You know I hate zombies."

"What are you talking about? You watched iZombie with me all the time?"

"Yeah, but she's just that one. And she knows what she's doing. Those things…ugh." She shuddered.

To the side of the couch were a pile of gifts I'd forgotten to unwrap while everyone was here. Karaoke was too lit, and I'd been having too much fun to care about what people got me. Plus, there was one from Naima in there. That made me that much more curious.

I ripped open a gift secured in bright wrapping paper to find a smartphone game made of a deck of cards. It required more than one person to play; otherwise, it was useless. Maybe I'd pull it out at work when I was on break with someone.

Gift number two was a sort of handheld wooden board with eight numbered keys made of tempered spring steel. I didn't know what it was, but Naima sure did. A mbira, or finger piano. I hit a few keys and was surprised how good I was at the first attempt. It was pretty dope. I'd have to remember to thank whoever got this one for me.

Naima cringed when I got to her gift, a small box wrapped in simple brown paper no bigger than a package you might find a cell phone in. I tossed it up in the air and caught it. It didn't weigh much, and as I did away with the gift wrap, it took taking it completely out of the packaging to uncover its purpose.

It was a USB car charger that was an eerie replica of the voice box, KITT, from the TV series *Knight Rider*. I'd never really watched the show, but I think my father was a fan of it. I remember the few times we'd spent time together, the show may or may not have been playing in the background. I pressed the button on top, bellowing a laugh at the familiar light sequence and programmed phrases that made that show famous.

"This is kind of funny. I like it. It should be a girl's voice, though. They should remake that series with, like, Scarlett Johansson's voice or better yet, Alicia Keys," I joked.

"I know it's stupid…"

"Naima, it's not stupid. I love it. Not every gift has to be well planned and thought-provoking. It's just nice to be thought of. Besides you'll probably see me charging my phone in this thing all the time. And now for the main event."

I pulled up the queued show to the main screen. Just as I planned to hit play, I stopped myself, knowing that Naima would only be here a little while longer. It was her voice I wanted to hear.

"On second thought, we don't have to watch this now. We can just hang out for a sec. I mean there's only, what, an hour or two before it gets so bad out where I can't take you home. Mind if we talk for a while? If not *The Walking Dead* awaits…"

She got comfortable and laid down on the far left end of the couch. "Let's see, zombies versus talking. I think I'll take my chances with the talking. I heard that show is scary, and I'm not trying to lose any sleep tonight."

"A grown-ass woman scared of a TV show. It's okay. I would've held your hand."

She kicked me in the side, then rested her popsicle-printed socked feet on the side of my leg.

"So what's up with you, Naima? What's new?"

She played with the string of her sweatpants as if unsure how to answer. "Everything's cool, I guess. Just pushing through and hanging on. That's all anyone ever does these days. But oh, looks like I have a plan after graduation. I'm moving to Baltimore. Not by myself, with my father. Just until I get on my feet, but you asked what's new."

Looking back at how crazy last year was for me, it was hard to process how much happened. Between us. Not between us. Pushing through and hanging on—nothing summed it up better than that. My spirit plummeted at the sound of her recent plans to move out of state. The time was getting close, and I was certain that what had happened between the two of us made it that much easier to come to that decision. Even if it wasn't about me, I had a feeling that once she was gone I'd never let myself believe that it wasn't.

"I want to ask...are we good? It feels like we've had this conversation a million times, but..." I rested my head in my hands. When you spend a lot of your nights alone, you have all this free time to look back at past choices. I'd be the first one to admit, when it came to her, I hadn't always made the right ones. I just didn't want that to be our entire history with each other. "It just seems like whenever we get to a good place, something happens. Or something doesn't happen. I know we've had what I'd describe as the wonkiest relationship, or friendship, or what-ever it is. But I want you to know that I'm really sorry. These past few months, they weren't me. My intention was never to hurt or disrespect you, and if I could take it back, I would. That's not the way I should've treated someone I care about. Thought you should know."

Her expression softened. "Tim, can I just say, I don't want to be at war any more than we have to be. My only wish is for us to get along. Which I believe we're working on right now." She laughed. Her palm met my shoulder in a smack as she laid back down. "Hey, what did you wish for? For your birthday, I mean. It took you forever to blow out those candles."

I took a deep breath. I knew what I wished for, but was I ready to be honest about it? I'd never been big on lying. With-holding information, maybe, but when someone wanted a real answer, I offered the truth.

"Oh, Naima, you don't want to know what I wished for."

"Oh, please, I'm not going to make fun of you. Everyone usually wishes for something they can't have. I'm sure you're no different."

That she was right about. What I wanted was out of my reach —or, at least, the way I wanted it. I wished for a way that she and I could make things work between us. And not just work but flourish. For us to both be equally great and together, without so much worry about what the future held. To have happier moments than sad ones, because let's face it, nothing was perfect and there were going to be sad ones. But that it wouldn't matter because we'd always work through them. I didn't wish for something spotless, just something real. Something that started and ended with her.

By now she was frustrated with my dodging the question. She'd declared a full-on attack on the side of my ribs by way of her fists. She wasn't hitting hard, so it was more annoying than painful, but it was getting to a point where, if I didn't pin her down, she'd go on like that for ten minutes straight. These girls from New York—they just thought they could go up against anyone. Not today.

In a quick, gentle swoop, I had Naima pressed against the couch as her arms wrestled with mine. "You really want to know what I wished for? Huh?" I said as she fought back hard. A feisty one she was. "Naima, you are not stronger than me," I taunted. But she still fought valiantly against the strongman hold. I recoiled when she managed to somehow kick me in the family jewels as she slithered away, laughing. "Shit, Naima. Why'd you even have to take it that far?" I groaned, clutching my goods.

Her smile faded as she kneeled over the back of the couch to see if I was okay. Rookie move.

I hopped over the back of the couch, and when it dawned on her that I was not, in fact, hurt, she took off in the direction of my bedroom. Her screams echoed as I snatched her up by the waist, binding her arms to her sides, unable to fight back.

"When will you learn that I'm the master of all tricksters? Grateful every day I have a face so damn trustworthy," I joked, steering her to the bed. She struggled in my grasp but gave up when she realized she wasn't going anywhere. I flipped her around, straddling her as I pinned her hands above her head with one hand, pointing with the other.

"You are a very naughty girl. Hope today's scuffle taught you something. That I cannot be bullied." I leaned in and kissed her cheek as my grip loosened on her wrists and I rolled onto the other side of her. "Birthday wish fulfilled."

She sat up, scooting over to me at the edge of the bed. "Well, if you wanted me back in your bed, you could have just asked. You didn't have to go through all that. Probably fucking up my hair and what not." She stroked her palms over her hair, her hands settling on the clasp of her right earring. The left was missing. Most likely lost in the onslaught.

The abrupt silence made even the faintest of sounds become suddenly more audible as the wind blew violently against my bedroom window. Her attention was lost to the area just above my bed and as I looked up I remembered it was her half to the painting we'd made together this past November. Under closer observation, it looked a little oddly situated with my room's muted color scheme. With its rich palette of rich purples and blues it just about contrasted everything but for that reason it reminded me of her. A distinctive piece in a room full of unimpressive objects.

"I can't believe you still have that hanging up."

I snickered. "It's like I told you before. Better than a good morning text." I said ending with a small laugh. Maybe I was doing it to myself holding onto it but I couldn't look at it without the recalling the memory of how it came to be. For that, I had no intention of taking it down.

"Hopefully, it's not so bad out to where I can't take you home. Are you just about ready to head out?"

She climbed on top of me, straddling me at the hips as she gathered her hair in her fist, pulling it out of her face. Our eyes met. Something about a person's eyes could tell you a lot of what they thought about. Eyes told stories. Eyes showed pain and loss, fear and excitement. There wasn't much you couldn't read in the way someone looked at you. But now, I couldn't make out one thing Naima's eyes wanted to tell me. For once since I'd known her, I hadn't a clue what was on her mind.

My palms stroked the outside of her thighs, finding comfort in how perfect they felt in my grasp. I counted on her to shake me off. Reject the intimate feel of my hands touching her, the same way she claimed she felt rejected by me. She didn't push me away.

No, she did something that only contributed to my already bewildered mind. She edged in close as her lips hovered over mine, her cool, tingly breathe prickling at the imprint of my mouth. Drunk in her spell, my lips savored the taste of her through the fury of that kiss.

"Wait." I pulled away, hesitant. "What are we doing here? We just…" I bit my bottom lip. "What are we doing?" As much as it pained me to stop, we were entering risky territory, and neither one of us had the common sense to hold back. Kissing her felt natural, and the way my heart raced, I didn't feel like stopping.

"No words…" she said enveloping, my mouth with hers. "Just this."

Our bodies pressed close, eager to indulge in each other for what could be the last time.

She eased her shirt over her shoulders as my hands rested on the indent of her waist. In this moment, she was beautiful. In this moment, she was mine. Even if only tonight. She covered my abdomen in electrifying kisses losing her patience to get me out of my clothes.

A low groan slipped past my lips when she teased my ear with her teeth but it was the bold caress of her tongue along my neck that made me rock hard. By the time she met me back at my mouth, my hands had found their way to her undergarments. She whimpered at the feel of my fingers gliding along her slick, sweet warmth, which required a thorough exploration of just how bad she wanted it. Wanted me.

Following my orders, she got on her hands and knees as I pulled her out of her panties. I wanted my tongue to be the reason she'd lose all five senses. I delved my tongue deep into her sweet spot, invoking cries of pleasure. The length of my tongue traveled up and down her sweet core. Her legs twitched with excitement when my palm came down hard on her ass, her moans high pitched and broken as my tongue swirled around her swollen clit.

She toyed with me, pulling away, then rubbing it in my face until she couldn't take it anymore. I locked my arms around her thighs to stop any unnecessary movement, feeding off her pleasure and wanting her to hold out to the very end. Her moans grew louder as she begged me to stop. But it only fueled my passion. High off the sounds she made and the taste of her sweet honey.

She growled in that familiar way she always did to let me know she was on her way to ecstasy as her body convulsed, trying desperately to break free of my hold. Her voice came out in muffled gasps as she bit into her pillow and balled the sheets up in her fists. Once again I slapped her ass, stroking my engorged cock in my other hand.

"Turn around, beautiful." As she twisted onto her back in a slow, seductive wiggle pressing her feet on top on my shoulders and later hooking her legs around my hips to reel me in. She washed her taste off my lips as the tip of her tongue fought with mine and circled onto my bottom lip.

It was easy to lose myself in this addiction known as Naima. The more I thought about it, the crazier it made me. There was no coming back from this time. I'd be fucked up forever.

Grabbing a condom from the nightstand, I met Naima with my craving lips, bracing myself for what could be my undoing. She pulled me close, guiding my hips to her opening. I opened my eyes to find Naima gazing back at me, her eyes reaching into my soul, adding intensity to the moment.

As she wrapped her legs around me, I found myself falling deeper and deeper in her tight depths, fighting hard to keep myself from losing my mind. Like gentle, mellow waves washing up along the surface, my force was slow and steady as the heat generating from our bodies closeness cast a light sheen of sweat along her exposed, flushed skin.

"Just like that." she whispered as my hips rocked back and forth against her delicate softness, going deeper with every thrust. As she edged toward her breaking point, every thrust felt hotter, tighter and wetter than the last.

"I'm about to come." Giving me just the jolt I needed to end things right on an explosive finish. I buried myself deep inside her, my hips molded into hers, driving her to the point of insanity. Her body tensed as her grip around me loosened, the walls of her center contracting on my ready to burst member.

With my final thrusts, a shockwave of built up tension ripped all the way through me in an earth shattering surrender. Out of breath and laced in sweat, I interlocked my fingers in hers as I reached in for one last sloppy kiss.

"Thanks for making this the best birthday I've ever had." I hopped up and slipped on a pair of basketball shorts as I looked out the window. The snow hadn't stopped and I knew if I waited until the morning to start shoveling the snow away from my car, I was going to regret it. I climbed back in bed with Naima. Some things would just have to wait. I wrapped my arms around her and nuzzled my chin in her neck.

"Mmm...I could sleep all day now. You sleepy?" She shrugged me off of her and reached for her clothes. "Sorry it's just, shit, no matter what I do or how much I avoid you, I always end up in your bed or in your car or anywhere else we manage to have sex. I tell myself it doesn't always have to be complicated. But it's like I can't friggin' kick you."

Not exactly the thing you want to hear after an in-heat moment. "Did you not want to?"

"That's the thing is that I did want to. I always want to. And that's my problem. I don't know how to not want to. Not with you."

It was only natural for two people who have this much history and chemistry to still be attracted to each other. I was always going to have a soft spot for her and I was never going to be able to think logically when she was around. But at least I didn't beat myself up over it. Feelings, they were what made us all human.

"For some dumb reason I thought I could do this. Prove to myself that you don't get under my skin. But now I'm just left feeling so out of place with literally nowhere else to turn until the morning."

"If it makes you feel any better, you can sleep on the couch…"

"I might just do that."

I grabbed her wrist before she could go any further. "Naima, please don't take me seriously." I sighed. "In the spirit of it being my birthday, is it possible to talk in detail after both of us are fully rested? Clear minds, time to reflect, maybe even over some breakfast. Is that cool?" She pursed her lips to the side.

"Yea, I guess we can do that." She rubbed at her temples, the stress and exhaustion wearing heavy on her face.

"Good. Relax. Let's get some sleep. All this other stuff can wait until the morning."

CHAPTER SIXTEEN

Naima

I woke up to an empty bed and the sounds of running water pinpointing Timothy's location. A lot of questions flooded my head, with no concrete answers as to why I was here. In Timothy's house. In Timothy's bed. I'd never thought of myself as one of those women who was so hung up on someone they couldn't let them go. In past relationships, I'd always been the master of decisions, maybe even a little bit of a heartbreaker. Not because it was the thing to do, but because I got bored easily with people who weren't the whole package.

Perhaps a guy matched my wits, but he didn't make me laugh. I didn't know how people could date someone with no sense of humor. Or maybe he was Nigerian (my mother's dream, despite remarrying an American man herself) and stylish, but too into himself and non-attentive to what I strived for in a relationship. The only answer that made sense to me was that everything I'd been looking for in a partner was what I saw, what I felt with Timothy.

He walked back into the room, his hair plastered to his forehead and a towel slung around his waist.

"All yours," he said as he handed me a towel.

"Think I could get something to put over my hair?" I asked, regretting not bringing along a scarf.

"I'll see what I have, but it's looking like I may only have, like, old grocery bags. Is that okay?" he said with a grin. It was going to have to do.

I'd been successful in finally getting around to putting some clothes on when the smell of maple, peppers, and breakfast sausage dragged me unwillingly to the kitchen. Timothy prepared two plates of something that looked like scrambled eggs, waffles, and meat. I sat at the table, knowing I wasn't much help at this stage. Everything was pretty much done, and plus I had all this shit on my mind.

"Timothy, is it just sex with you or do you actually still have feelings for me?"

At that, he laughed. "Always the first one in the pool." He laid down a plate in front of me.

"It's a yes or no question."

He set his plate down across from my chair, headed in the direction of the utensil drawer. "Naima, please. Neither one of us has had any food yet, or at least coffee."

He pointed me in the direction of a fresh pot brewing. I poured us both a mug full and brought them to the table.

"Thank you," he said as I parked my butt in my seat and scooted closer to the table.

A few bites of those eggs and I was in heaven. "Wow, this is so good."

He smiled. "Yeah, I discovered Pinterest. Now *that* is a death trap." He was always an expert at making me laugh. I swear I hated that about him.

"So I asked you a question."

"And I owe you an answer, but…here, let's do it like this. You wanted to talk, so talk. Once you get some things off your chest, I'll chime in."

Now that the moment was here, I was so nervous. Why did he make me so nervous? "So…these past few months…last night… I'm not sure what this all is. I thought that this was what I wanted. To have sex. To prove to myself that I was finally done with you. To convince myself that it was possible for it to only be sex between us. But I realized that…I don't want that to be the kind of friendship we have. Maybe we aren't as close as we used to be and I'm not here to play the blame game, but there was a time you were my best friend. That is what I want. You made living in a new place feel a lot less lonely, and that's what I want back. What we just did, what we keep doing—it's always everything it used to be, but I don't think I can handle it all without the promise of something concrete. Either we're friends who don't fuck, or we're more than just friends. Timothy, say something."

He shrugged. "I'm listening."

"That's it. That's what I had to say."

He took a bite of his food and answered after he swallowed. "You sure?" I nodded. What else was left to say? Timothy brought his hands together in a clap. He leaned into the table on his elbows and scooted in closer.

"Last spring, I hated you. You had me so fucked up to the point where it took every ounce of something I didn't have just to look at you. Which is hard to do when you work together, but the way you ended things, I'm not going to lie, I was so fuckin' bitter. I think what changed was when you left RI to go back home for the summer. I spent three months not being able to stop thinking about you. Then you came back when school started back up, and that's when I knew it wasn't you I hated—it was our situation. I'm not calling myself perfect. Every day I work on trying to be a better version of myself. But when I came to you, ready to commit myself entirely to you, you shit on me. And that hurt. Naima, your friendship is everything to me. And making love to you is probably the only way to end an amazing day, but if you ask me right now, I am very reluctant to attach myself to something serious with you. I hope you can understand…"

Honesty. We say we want it, but when we get it, we get our feelings hurt. Hearing him say those things was hard. I even surprised myself for keeping it together without showing much emotion. Not the words I'd been looking for. Not by a long shot.

"I respect you keeping it real with me, Tim—"

He pressed his fingers to my lips, requesting that he take the floor. "Just so things are perfectly clear. I never stopped having feelings for you. I meant everything I ever told you. Especially when I told you that I loved you. I still do. So imagine seeing you at work, every day, trying to pretend like I don't. You get into my system because that's what you do, that's what you're good at, and then I can't free myself of you. I want you all the time, and I don't think of what *could* happen or what *will* happen. I only think about the way you make me feel, and that's not always a good thing. Even now, I can't have you like I want to, and the situation just sucks."

He loved me. Even after all the drama we'd been through—all that avoiding each other at work, all that uncomfortable small talk—Timothy still loved me. The rules had changed and the terms were set. No longer on the same page, but on the next chapter. Nothing stood in our way this time. We could be open. We could be normal. We could be us.

We could be us.

"Can't we just start over?"

He took a deep breath, resting his fist in his palm. "Naima, six months from now, where do you plan to be? I mean, after you graduate?"

The thought never occurred to me until now, but if I hadn't made the decision to move to the DMV with my father, with nothing going on for me here I would've probably moved back home. Rhode Island was always supposed to be temporary. I'd never thought about making a permanent life here. Come June, I'd be in Baltimore, looking for a job closer suited to my degree.

"I hadn't thought of that." I lowered my head, not sure of what to say to make light of the topic at hand.

"What happens when you leave Rhode Island for good? Where does that leave me? The last five years all over again. Naima, I want a girlfriend who's going to be around when I want to see her. Willing to make the sacrifices I'd make for her. Someone who'll laugh with me. Laugh at me. Smoke with me. Curl up next to me when we've both had hard days. I know New York isn't far, but it's still a distance. I want something different with you. Better. And I know you can't promise me that."

There was a silence between us, and I couldn't find the words to argue with all the points he'd made. He was so right it hurt. I couldn't promise him anything.

"Naima, please don't be mad at me."

I wasn't mad. Especially not the way he made me see things. It was one of the things I really dug about him. He was able to make me see things from a different perspective. He was so good at getting his point across. I only wished our situation was differ- ent. We were perfect for each other in our own imperfect little way. I respected his decision and had to accept that being friends was all we'd ever be. Right now, I just needed a friend.

"Are we still cool?" he asked, holding out his fist for me to bump.

"Still cool."

CHAPTER SEVENTEEN

Naima

The day had finally come after six years of putting it off and two years in a place far from where I called home. I was actually doing it. *Graduating*. Had I had known it'd feel this good, I would've done it years ago when the pressure was on and the support was there.

But this moment, this time I'd spent working on this chapter of my life, was about to unfold. And it all started with me walking across that stage when the called my name to accept that piece of paper.

Turning back into the massive crowd, it was easy to spot both my mother and father sitting next to one another, getting along and occasionally stealing a glance my way as if to silently say, "Yea, you see. We did that." Though no longer together, it was nice to see them come out in support of their only daughter without any Jerry Springer outbursts. My dad in his tailored purple caftan and matching slim fit pants and my mom wearing an identical ensemble made up of purple blouse and wrapper with the most elegantly tied Ichafu adorned on her head were the definition of the what it meant to 'show up' and had me beating myself up for not going for something traditional under my gown.

I would've loved to stand out in a sea of wavy hair and knee length formal wear but I'd spent all weekend splurging on the prefect two-piece skirt set, a splash of an island-like pink that complemented the stunning shade I was born into. I couldn't wait to do away with this gown, though. How was it only May and already 85?

I looked all over the place to find the only people missing were my friends. Because I hadn't had many tickets to go around after inviting my parents and their spouses, the only ones willing to shell out an extra twenty bucks for an extra ticket were my closest friends at work, Angel, Ruby, Emily and who could forget Timothy.

The past three months had been a strong test of our friendship with things going back to normal for the two of us, whatever that was supposed to mean. It was as if we never had that messy spat so long ago. Work was fun again. We, were fun again; as much as it hurt not to have him in my life the way I'd hoped things would work themselves out, I was grateful just to have my best friend back. People like him were a rare find and I knew somewhere down the line that man was going to make a willing someone a very lucky woman one day. I only hoped we were still good friends long enough for me to see it happen.

The four finally came into view as my name was called and I made haste up the five-step staircase to glide across the stage, praying I didn't trip on my way to shake hands with the university's president. Any other day hearing my friends chanting my name over an already deafening crowd of people would have been slightly embarrassing, it was nice knowing I actually had friends here to share this day with me. I was beyond blessed.

After the last leg of the ceremony, I took off to meet my mother and father, who were both waiting for me at the end of the stage. I embraced them both in a hug that eventually included both of their spouses. It got a little more crowded after my cousin and stepbrother felt left out and added on to the circle, aware yet unbothered that they were squeezing the life out of me.

"You guys, you're going to have to ease up a little. You're all crushing me." And they did, but it was my father who refused to stop talking. He was so proud that his baby girl had finally graduated and was the happiest I'd seen him in a long time.

"Baba, calm down, will you? I'm not running for president. I'll be that, if you want to throw a couple hundred thousand my way for a campaign. For that I'd highly consider it." I chortled. As my mother approached me from the side, she handed me a plain envelope out of her oversized handbag.

"What's this, ma?" I asked curiously, but lost my patience and ripped it open before she could properly explain.

"It's a gift from your father and I. Try to do something responsible with it, like buy a car. I am told that you need a car to navigate Maryland." My mouth dropped. In front of me stood a cashier's check in the generous amount of sixty-two hundred dollars with my name on it. My folks didn't just have spare money lying around; both had their own families, households and expenses they were in charge of. I almost felt bad knowing they most likely had to cut a lot of corners to make this gift happen but as long as I've been their daughter I knew if they were both giving me something, it meant they wanted me to have it. Trying to offer things back to her annoyed the hell out of my mother, so I didn't even bother. To her, it was as if you assumed she didn't have it to give. No, this money wouldn't buy me a brand new car but it *would* get me something more reliable than a beater.

I wrapped my arms around her waist, my head taking refuge on her chest. "Thanks, ma. You and Baba are the best."

"Eh, just don't waste it, okay?" she said with a kiss to my forehead. She alerted me in her native tongue that the girl she'd met last January, along with an odd group of mostly white people (or what she'd gathered were white from first glance) were staring at us and my mind immediately went to Ruby and the others.

"Oh, them? Those are the friends I've made here."

She sneered. "Well tell them not to stand there and stare. We do not bite." And she was absolutely right, she didn't bite. She tore you to shreds if you gave her the chance to.

"Ma, be nice."

"I'm always nice." She retorted with a slight frown on her face. That was *her* version of nice.

"I'm going to go over there and talk to them all really quick. Then I'll introduce everyone. Is that fine?" As I waited for my parents to nod before I sauntered over to the four, thoroughly impressed they found the occasion worthy enough to dress up for it. I didn't think it was worth all the effort but how nice was it that they deemed it important enough to do so.

Emily looked sweet (a nice change) in her yellow, floral sundress while Ruby kept it trendy with her cobalt blue strapless jumpsuit. Newly single for less than a month and the girl was pulling no stops to get over Lisette. I had to admit it was weird being in the middle of their breakup but it couldn't have been any different than how Ruby had felt when she went back and forth between me and Timothy. At least with them it was mutual. Ruby understood that once Lisette made plans to commit to a one-year internship and on top of that a three-year residency, she just wouldn't have the time she had before to dedicate to a serious relationship. Either way, she was fighting the loneliness—while looking fabulous on the regular. We'd actually gotten around to having a girls' night with just the two of us. I had to confess that single, she was far more fun.

And how could I forget the boys, all cleaned up and dapper in their dress shirts and chinos, both looking remarkably handsome.

"Look at all of you getting all dressed up for little ole' me." One by one they all showered me with hugs.

"Well, you know. We didn't want to embarrass you or anything." Angel said with a roll of his eyes. "Plus we weren't sure if you had something going on after this. We know it's your last day in Providence and all. We can't let you leave without seeing you off." Angel finished.

"Well…" I said glancing back at my family. "Let me see what my folks want to do and if they're trying to go out, we could meet up later instead. In the meantime, allow me to introduce you to my dysfunctional ass family."

They followed me over and between reciting the names of ten or so people, in five minutes flat everyone knew everyone. My father (*bless him*) was his usual warm, welcoming self. My mother on the other hand? Firm on handshaking and less on smiling. Her version of nice I had to remind myself. *Her* version of nice.

"Where is the best place to take my daughter and her friends out to celebrate? Beverages and lunch are all on me." My father announced in his rich accent. I looked between my friends' confused faces before stepping in to make a comment.

"Okay so one y'all better start talking before my father changes his mind, be it Indian or Italian, hell even Denny's. This sort of thing doesn't happen every day and I don't know about you, but I'm starving."

Ruby and Emily both had their suggestions but it was Angel and Tim's idea that sounded the most appealing.

"Hey, there's this Peruvian spot Angel and I ate at a few weeks ago. Great for full houses. We shared this one plate that we could barely finish. What was that spot called?" Tim started.

"Machu Picchu" Angel filled in the blanks. "Yea, Machu Picchu. They give you *so* much food. With a party this size that's our best bet." Tim said. When no one could disagree, it was decided. Peruvian it was.

As we all dispersed into separate cars, I took my chances

riding with Tim and Emily after Angel's arrangements felt a bit crowded when my niece invited herself to ride with him and Ruby.

Ruby and my cousin had really hit it off that time Ruby came into New York with me, so I suppose she was just tired of listening to my mom's Christian stations opting instead to be around younger people with similar musical tastes to her own. I just wanted to spend this last day with my friends knowing this might be the last time in a long time we'd all sit down and do something together. I wasn't sure how often I'd be back but I was positive that if I ever did return, Staten Island would be a person of the past, a faded memory replaced by someone as equally likable but ten times more charming.

Naima, stop it. You're supposed to be having fun. It could be a while before I relived this sort of fun when I was down in Maryland, friendless and with no damn job. I took one deep breath, remembering that there was a lot to accomplish in a foreign place.

When the rear door slammed shut, I looked up from my lap to see we'd arrived at the restaurant and Emily was making her way to meet up with the others who'd managed to get here before us. Timothy pulled up his emergency park before turning off his car.

"Before you get out, I was wondering. You still needed my help getting your stuff from your apartment, right?" I clicked off my seatbelt casting my gaze in his direction. I hoped he hadn't planned on bailing on me but if he was, with Angel here, I suppose it wouldn't hurt to enlist him.

"I don't have that much stuff, Tim. If something's come up I could always get my dad or Angel to help out. I know you probably have tons of things to do."

"No, I was just making sure you still needed me. There was something I wanted to talk to you about anyways. I'll just wait until then."

"Umm, are you sure? Because you might hate me after lugging

all my shit around. I'd rather you just get it out the way now." His face contorted into a grimace, as he tilted his head back and forth weighing his options.

"Nah, it can wait. Don't want to keep your family waiting. Who seem great by the way. No big deal, just don't forget to remind me. I've been up since five so you know how worthless I can be when I haven't gotten any sleep." I rolled my eyes.

"Fine, and when you do show up you better not drop by empty handed. Ruby bought me a make-up kit. Angel got me flowers. Hell, even Em got me a damn gift card and that girl is always broke." He laughed.

"Naima, I did get you something. The only reason I haven't given it to you is because I didn't want to show off in front of everyone else making their gifts seem all inadequate. But I guarantee you it's nice, I promise."

"Oh you know I'm only joking with you. You didn't have to get my anything."

"Yea, I know but I wanted to. Now c'mon let's go. I think your mom is giving us the evil eye for making everyone wait out in this heat." I looked ahead at everyone gathering in front of the restaurant and sure enough my mom was burning a hole through the glass like she caught me skimming money out the collection plate at her church. It was a look that just two months' shy of my twenty-ninth birthday I should've been immune to but that look still brought fear in me. I'd be sure to sit on the end where my father was sitting, where the mood would be lighter with his bad-joke-telling skills. My dad, bless him, didn't know the meaning of a punch line. He was always giving it away in the middle of the joke and I vowed to make everyone else fans of the terrible jokes I'd grown up loving.

Joining up with the rest of our party we were quickly seated upon arrival, my family skipping every other seat as a chance to chat up someone new from my circle of friends. A rainstorm of panic trickled through me when Timothy chose to sit next to my mom, all the way on the *other* side of the table. After all, I'd never told my mom about anyone I'd met here, let alone someone I *sort of* dated. All it would take were a few invasive questions about his personal life and my mom became Matlock putting each little piece together.

The upside to that was that Tim and I were only friends now, so there wasn't anything to really put together. Still, there was no telling what either one would say once a sangria pitcher started going around, but I had to remind myself that I was always tense over the smallest things when I didn't have any food in my stomach.

"Can I start you all with something to drink?" a waiter on my side asked in broken English. He released a sigh of relief when I eased his nerves by answering back in Spanish, something my father to this day held me in high regard for taking the time out to learn. Between going back and forth with Angel, who'd been here before and the only other Spanish speaker at the table, we'd agreed on the Jalea Familiar, the largest platter of delectably fried seafood designed just for a group our size. If this was my last meal in Rhode Island, it had better be the best thing I tried since I got here. The last thing I needed was for a terrible meal to spoil my memory of living here.

What am I saying? These people, my friends and family, they were all here for me. When I thought about it like that, there wasn't anything, not even bad food I could think of that could spoil this amazingly good time.

"The door's open." I yelled out after hearing the knock on the door. Without Lisette's primitive decorations, the room looked scarcely plain and bones bare. Even with my clothes out the closet, the place was beginning to look more and more like a base apartment. I was lucky to have only brought clothes with me while living here, so my nine boxes looked like nothing compared to the moving truck Lisette enlisted to manage all her things out.

Thank god I never brought anything more than I needed; although thinking about it, I had about twice as many clothes now than I'd had a year ago. And two of these boxes that were shamelessly hoarding hair products certainly wasn't pleading my case. #confessionsofaproductjunkie

Tim popped his head in my old room offering to hold a boxes flap down as I secured it shut with tape. "Your stuff isn't too bad. For some reason, I thought you were going to have boxes on top of boxes, but I think we can manage it all in one trip if I bring my seats down. We'll see."

Like me, he'd dressed down to something more casual from earlier. A slim fit Henley and jeans, probably predicting to be up to his waist in boxes. Why did he always look so handsome even when he hadn't put any effort? Maybe I'd never stop finding him attractive. As much as I loved to put things in the past where they belonged, I still held a place in my heart for him and probably always would but I had nothing going on for me right now. The wisest thing for me to do was to pick up and start over in a new place just as I had done two years ago when I moved to Providence.

I had no apartment, an embarrassing four hundred dollars in my bank account (although my parents gift today would bring me up to sixty-six hundred) and as of two days ago once I'd put in my two week notice, I was without a job. There wasn't anything I could really offer anyone at this point but a smile and a piece of paper that would take six weeks for them to mail to me. I needed to be somewhere I could restart my life and right now, I wasn't sure Rhode Island was the place to do it. Not without a job or a place to live. I couldn't be there for Tim the way he wanted me to and I loved him so much that I only wanted his happiness. Even if that meant that another woman would be the one that made him happy.

"You know, Tim. I really appreciate you helping me get all my stuff out of here and letting me keep it at your house until I get ready to get out of here. I only had until today to get my stuff out of here." He smiled, that charming smile that when I first met him, I knew I'd always be a sucker for.

"Alright, I feel a hug coming on. Let's just get it out of the way before things get all wet and emotional." He said as he pulled me in for a tight embrace. For the moment we stood there with his arms wrapped around me, my vision flooded with a dozen or so memories to where I'd always felt safe in his arms. I was never going to meet another person like him. That both confused and intrigued me. I was going to miss me some Timothy Ferreiro. *Mr. Ferreiro, if you were nasty.*

"That's what friends do for each other." He said as he lifted me up from the floor before putting me back down. "Besides, I've got some places to stop before we get to my house and because you owe me one, I'm going to need you to keep the car running and hit your foot on that gas when I say so. No questions asked."

"You are so stupid." I pushed him away, laughing, trying to keep a level head. I hated being that close to him. Not without thinking we were the best thing that never was. The way he felt, the way he made me smile; trying hard not to expose the overwhelming feelings that came over me, I wiped away the few tears that managed to leave my eyes and traveled down my cheek but I wasn't fast enough. He'd already caught me in the act.

"Naima you're not crying, are you?"

"No." I lied.

"*Naima.*"

"No, stupid, I'm not crying. It's that damn cologne you got on. Making my eyes water and shit. Like, damn, are you helping me move or meeting up with someone after this?" He picked up a box and headed straight to the door.

"Yea, okay," he added with suspicion. "I'm going to get started on loading up my car. Assuming that I'm helping you and not just doing all the moving, *I* will see you outside."

❧

I laid the last box from his car next to the other eight boxes in a corner in Timothy's living room. After three exhausting trips back and forth with those heavy ass boxes, I was ready to pass out on his loveseat.

"You don't mind if I get something to drink, do you?" I asked.

"Go ahead." He answered back as he disappeared in the back to his bedroom. I grabbed a bottle of water and as I walked back out to the living room, he was sitting on the couch fiddling with the buttons on one of his PS4 controllers.

"Mind if I chill out for a little while? I'm not really looking forward to spending the night at Ruby's. It's cool when her family's asleep but when they aren't, everyone is so damn loud. I just want a dose of peace and quiet before that long drive in the morning. My dad, stepmom and stepbrother with all their different musical tastes, it's going to be hell to my ears." He leaned back on the couch.

"You know I'm not going to tell you no. Stay as long as you like. Just, if I happen to fall asleep, just wake me up."

I sat down on the opposite side of the couch, laughing the second a thought I'd been sitting on all night trying to remember to bring up.

"Hey," I poked him in the side with my foot. He tilted his head toward me with sleepy dark brown eyes and a slack expression. "Hmm?"

"You know what my mom told me today?" I cleared my throat, prepping my voice for my best Ngozi Anderson impression. "She goes, *That friend of yours, the white boy. He is a charmer of words. Men like that, you must watch them closely.*" I imitated in her accent. "No matter how much I begged she wouldn't tell me. So now that I have you here, I want to know what you said to her." He laughed, avoiding my eyes as he stared up at the ceiling.

"You really want to know what I told her?"

"Yes, because she was *almost* smiling and anyone who knows my mom would know that's a rare occasion. I'm talking Nigeria qualifying for the world cup—rare occasion." He sat up a little straighter, this time meeting my eyes as he bit his lip. "I told your mother I was going to make her daughter my wife one day and if I did, would I have her blessing?" *This idiot.* Always playing.

"No, for real, Tim. What did you tell her?"

"You want to know what I told her, *that's what I told her.*" Well damn, no wonder she was laughing. That was the sort of thing you couldn't joke around about with a foreign mother involved. Especially not mine. According to her, I was well beyond my expiration date to get hitched up. About five years past, something she constantly reminded me of. It was hard keeping a straight face, especially considering what my mother thought of the gesture but Timothy wasn't laughing with me.

"Oh c'mon Tim, it's funny. I'm laughing see." I pointed to my grinning mouth.

"Okay, and who said I was joking?" he said causing my laughter to cease.

"Well, I mean for one we're just friends—"

"No Naima, we're not. We're friends who are in love with each other. There's a huge difference. I know you still love me, but I also know you're too selfless to leave me brokenhearted again. That, I appreciate." His hand traveled down his face, the stress of the topic making him look more tired than he was. He rested his hand on the top of my ankle.

"You know Ruby and I were talking a few weeks back, a little after her split with Lisette. I was just asking her if she still thought about her. And if she could do something differently to convince her to stay, would she have? She told me no. That they would've worked out if they were meant to and it just had me thinking. Mostly about how hard it is to let someone you love walk out your life like that. Speaking from experience, it's been the hardest thing I've ever had to do and now that the time is coming again, I'm terrified. Terrified of missing you. Terrified of losing you. I just…" he hesitated. "I just like myself better when I have the pleasure of being around you."

I was not hearing this—not with tomorrow being my last day here in Providence. Why did he choose now to make it that much harder to say goodbye?

"Why are you telling me this now?"

"Better now than when you're five states away." He scouted in closer and lifted my chin to meet his face, sincerity painting his expression into an invisible veil of desperation mixed in with hope.

"I'm not ready to let you go yet. Not now." He said with slight hesitation in his voice. It was then that I noticed him pulling something out of his pocket. A small, velvet ring box.

"No one can promise someone forever, but whatever time I have left in this life, I want it to be with you." He opened up the box and sitting there cozy in plush lining was a solitaire ring crafted in white gold with a glittering round cut diamond that was the biggest cut I'd ever seen this up close.

"Now you're just staring at me. I don't know if that's a good thing." *Dammit, was I really staring?* My thoughts were up in the air right now and the only thing I could process was that this man was really proposing to me right now. For the past three months we hadn't taken part in any overstepped boundaries. For the first time since we'd known each other we were just that— friends looking out for one another. And now this.

I was at a loss for words, or perhaps I'd lost the ability to speak. All I knew was Timothy was waiting for me to say something and I couldn't predict what that something might be.

"Naima, don't make me start singing. Because once I start

singing, you'll be compelled to say yes, especially since I'll hit all those notes you like and all sexy-like too— "

"Yes—" I blurted out, surprised to finally hear that my voice did indeed work.

"Yes?"

"Yes, I want to be with you. Spend my life with you. Marry you. Yes, to everything it entails." He jerked back with one eyebrow cocked as a smile formed at the corner of his lips that then spread to the length of his mouth.

"Really?" he said releasing a deep breath. "Wow, I think my heart just stopped. *You said yes.* I was really hoping you would say —" I pressed my lips against his, letting all the uncertainty drain away with that one kiss. I'd accepted that the road ahead for me was complicated but the feelings I had for this man was just about the only thing I was sure of these days. We owed it to ourselves to test this relationship out for the long run. We could be different than before. Better. And now I didn't have to risk the chance of asking myself if never giving us a shot would be the biggest mistake I'd ever made.

"Mmm…that was nice. You have no idea how much I missed those lips." As he leaned in again to kiss me, this time with an intense degree of patience and a skilled level of passion.

"Hey, I have an idea." He said climbing on top of me as he wrestled to pull my shirt over my head. "How about we get started on those beautiful babies…"

I knew that he was joking but the moment this all starting setting in, I'd just realized something. My parents were still in town and I knew for a fact that they'd kill me if I let them go all the way home without telling them why I *wouldn't* be leaving tomorrow with my father.

"Wait, umm. While my folks are still here, we have to tell them. Although you've already met, they're going to want to know more about you. Because…*reasons.*"

"Okay, well we can do all that tomorrow. What you fail to

realize is for the past three months I've been without you so I'm going to need a crash course on all things Naima Adewunmi."

"Yea well, pretty soon it'll be Mrs. Ferreiro. But that's only if you're nasty." I tittered. By now, he became impatient to how slow my clothes left my body.

"Oh, I'm totally nasty. Filthy even. I'm about to show you all night how much of a dirty boy I've been. Now c'mere you." He whisked me up in his arms, carrying me over to his bedroom (*or maybe now it was our bedroom?*) as he leaned in to give me one last peck before leaving me with one last thought.

"Naima, there has never been a woman alive that has ever made me feel the way you make me feel. Thank you for making me the happiest man on the planet."

Thanks so much for making it all the way to the end of part two of Tim and Naima's story! We so hope you devoured it! Before you go, we'd love if you could leave a few short words of what you thought of Next Chapter!

Follow this link to review and tell others what you thought. Again, thank you for your purchase and be sure to flip through the end pages to discover more addictive reads from G.L. Tomas. Happy Reading!

ACKNOWLEDGMENTS

Who do we thank first? Obviously our editor, Rebecca! We kind of do a happy dance whenever we hear from her and work ·with her!
We've gotten some really positive feedback from readers with *Same Page*, and I don't think we would've had the guts to finish *Next Chapter* if it hadn't been for them! We know certain subjects are difficult for readers, and it was scary to release a book that started with a man who was unfaithful to his girlfriend. But with what we've learned from writing these books, we were able to apply those thoughts and ideas to future works, so hopefully they will connect with readers that much more!

Don't forget to sign up for our newsletter for new releases and messy romances—you won't regret it, loves. Sign up <u>here</u>.

ABOUT THE AUTHOR

G.L. Tomas is a twin writing duo and lover of all things blerdy, fearless and fun. When they're not spending their time crafting swoon-worthy heroes, they're battling alien forces in other worlds but occasionally take days off in search mom and pop spots that make amazing pasteles and tostones fried to perfection.

They host salsa lessons and book boyfriend auditions in their secret headquarters located in Connecticut.
Head over to our Official website @ GLTomaswrites.com There we have a list of our upcoming titles and you can purchase our paperbacks directly, along with other swag!

Sign up for G.L. Tomas' newsletter.

You'll get exclusives, such as book release updates, chances to win or earn free swag, access to well thought-out book lists, and opportunities to save on books before anyone else!

Don't forget to connect with us on Bookbub and our exclusive Facebook Group! And be sure to send us an email to talk books and about your fave characters! Drop us a line at guinevere.libertad@gltomaswrites.com

If you liked reading *Next Chapter* as much as we did writing it, please consider leaving a review! Reviews are a huge part of how other readers discover and judge a book. It may seem like such a small gesture but it's a small gesture that goes a long way and makes the book you loved come up in more also bought searches and has the chance to be featured in consumer newsletters.

Just a quick "I loved this book" is praise enough and encourages your favorite writers to churn out that next favorite read. So don't be shy, if you enjoyed reading, a review would mean the world for a relatively new book! You can do so by clicking here.

Evan Cattaneo was used to getting what he wanted.

The successful career. **Check.**

The Penthouse apartment overlooking the city. **Check.**

Let's not forget the drop-dead gorgeous girlfriend. **Triple Check.**

Only now, being in the relationship of his dreams, he discovers one slight problem that puts a dent in his plans for the future. His girlfriend Luz doesn't see herself getting hitched.

Forcing Evan to confront their differences and understand their conflicting ideas.

The Engagement Plan.

A trip across the country, some much-needed therapy and their ability to work together as a couple fit into that neat little package. Only the closer he comes to uncovering the truth behind her reasons, he learns a devastating secret that will affect the state of their once happy union.

<u>Pre-order now!</u>

Leomie Coutard was looking to create a fresh start. New place, new job prospects, the task she's yet to conquer? Her non-existent love life. Considering her unique taste, sadly, not just any guy would do.

She met the man of her dreams presenting at a kink conference a year ago, but being oceans apart forced their two-week long connection to come to an end. Or did it?

Damien Karagiannis couldn't believe his luck. Settling into a different country and a new practice left him less time to meet people, let alone date. Through a wicked twist of fate, he not only gets the chance to reconnect to his budding Dominant stranger through matchmaker Mistress Alice she ends up being a part of his surgical team.

Leomie can't get the intimidatingly sexy surgeon out of her system. Damien craves that soft command he once explored. Their undeniable passion will have them breaking all their rules for each other.

Melt For You is a steamy May/December romance that features a gentle Domme with an appetite for masochism and an arrogant yet romantic male submissive who wants nothing but to make her wishes come true. It is BWWM with no cheating and a guaranteed HEA. If Dominance and submission aren't your style, sit this one out. If you like a little kink, let this Alpha submissive melt his way into your heart!

Pre-order now!

ALSO BY G. L. TOMAS

Love Unexpected Series:

Love finds even those not looking!

The Love Bet

The Engagement Plan(Pre-order now)

The Hook-Up Games (sign up to our mailing list to learn more!)

Kinky Matchmaker Series:

Kinksters find their perfect naughty match!

Meant For You

Melt For You (Available for Pre-order)

More For You(sign up to learn when it drops)

Friends That Have Sex Series:

A love pessimist and gentle bad boy can't get enough of each other...

F*THS (Also available in audio)

Friends That Still... (Also available in audio)

Friends That Collide (sign up to learn when it drops)

Bookish Friends To Lovers Series:

Book lovers find they have more than enough in common to take it there despite the circumstances.

Same Page (Also available in audio)

Next Chapter

Pagebreak (sign up to learn when it drops)

Bookmark (sign up to learn when it drops)

www.ingramcontent.com/pod-product-compliance
Lightning Source LLC
Chambersburg PA
CBHW050352190726
48284CB00007BB/2257